PRETTY AS A PICTURE

If you saw me on the street, you might
recognize me. It's not that I'm a famous
celebrity or anything like that, but sometimes
people remember my face from TV and they
say, "Hey, weren't you the kid that got
knocked over by the St. Bernard in the dog-
food commercial?" Mostly they remember the
Coco Balm commercial, though, and nine times
out of ten, they'll even remember the lines
I spoke and the music they played in the
background. I guess that's the commercial
that will stick out in my head the rest of my
life, too.

Everybody asks me how I got started. And
how come I'm not driving in my own Silver
Cloud, behind a chauffeur, instead of in my
parents' old red Toyota.

"I've lent my Rolls to the President," I tell
them. As for the rest, it's a long story.

**Other Scholastic paperbacks
you will enjoy:**

ADORABLE SUNDAY

Marlene Fanta Shyer

AN
APPLE®
PAPERBACK

SCHOLASTIC INC.
New York Toronto London Auckland Sydney

ISBN 0-590-40771-6

12 11 10 9 8 7 6 5 4 3 2 1   6 7 8 9/8 0/9

Printed in the U.S.A.   01

To Alison,
my adorable data bank

ADORABLE SUNDAY

1

IF you saw me on the street, you might recognize me. It's not that I'm a famous celebrity or anything like that, but sometimes people remember my face from TV and they say, "Hey, weren't you the kid that got knocked over by the St. Bernard in the dog-food commercial?," or "Weren't you the kid hanging out of the treehouse waving a frozen yogurt on a stick?" Mostly they remember the Coco Balm commercial, though, and nine times out of ten, they'll even remember the lines I spoke and the music they played in the background. I guess that's the commercial that will stick out in my head the rest of my life, too.

Everybody asks me how I got started. And when I got started. And how much I make. And how come I'm not driving in my own Silver Cloud, behind a chauffeur, instead of in my parents' old red Toyota.

"I've lent my Rolls to the President," I tell them. As for the rest, it's a long story.

I generally say it all started right after Dr. Mulkhoff took off my top and bottom braces and my mother saw my teeth all lined up straight for the first time in their lives, but I really think it goes back much further than that, like to the day I was born.

My mother looked at my bald head and decided I was going to be some kind of Judy Garland/Shirley Temple/Aileen Quinn or something, and she told my father I should not go through life with an ordinary name like everyone else. I was supposed to have been named Jane, after my grandmother in Arizona, and Elizabeth, after my grandmother in Illinois, so my father thought having had me had been too much for her brain. "Sunday is a day of the week, not a child," he said, "Besides, she was born today, and today is Thursday."

"Sunday is a special day, and this is going to be a special child," my mother said. "I can't help when she was born."

So I became Sunday Donaldson, and for about thirteen years after that, nothing much happened except we got my brother, Edward, who wound up with a normal name (he was named after a king, no relation), and we moved to a bigger house when my dad changed companies. He is with Consolidated Data Products now, covering the entire east coast, including Maine and Florida, and selling home computers that can do everything from predicting what the stock market will do tomorrow to looking up your uncle's number in the telephone book. Next year we may get one of our own, but in the meantime Dad said for entertainment we would have to make do with our color television set and the big tank of tropical fish in the den.

The fish really belong to Edward, who wanted something with four legs, but he's allergic to decent animals like dogs and cats and mice and gerbils. For a kid who had his heart set on a schnauzer, Edward has really adapted very well to fish. In fact, if he's not talking about them, he's talking to them, and when he isn't talking to them, he's cleaning filters, adjusting the reflectors, or throwing fish food in the northeast corner of the tank (according to instructions in one of his fish books), or asking my mother to turn up the heat because the fish look cold.

Edward also eats chocolate-covered bananas on sticks (his favorite food), different flavors of marshmallows, and peanut butter out of the jar, direct, which drives both Mom and Dad crazy. "Edward the King did not do those things, or he would not have fit on his throne" is the way my father puts it. "I'll encourage him to cut down" is the way my mother handles it. In any case, Edward is too round for Little League, for track, or for TV commercials, so he's underfoot a lot. I keep telling him if I were a candy freak I would never have gotten into the television commercial world.

He says one big, shining star in a family is enough. I tell him one little brother in a family is enough, but the truth is, as little brothers go, I've seen worse. He covers up for me (like when I lost my library book and he hid the letter from the school librarian until I could find the book), he lends me money (three dollars and forty cents for a birthday party gift last week), and he puts out the trash for me the nights I'm busy working on book reports or studying French verbs. My friend Karen's brother monopolizes the phone and shortsheets her bed and hides her hairbands to be funny. Edward wouldn't do that; fortunately, he's too busy with his Dwarf Gouramis, Blue Bettas, and Sumatran Barbs.

It was at Edward's ninth birthday party that my career actually got under way. He had this big cake (which he wanted to eat all the flowers off right away), and Dad got the old Polaroid out and began running around saying, "Hold it!" "Smile!" "Look up!" and snapping Edward and me and the three kids Mom had invited to Edward's party, and suddenly Mom grabbed one picture of me and got very excited. In the picture I was holding a balloon, and she brought it out to the kitchen where the light is good so she could get a better look.

"Doesn't she look adorable?" she asked Dad, who'd come in for more ice cubes for the punch.

"Adorable!" Edward snickered, having big ears that could pick up things all the way from the dining room. "Just plain *adorable!*"

"With her braces off—look! She could really model now."

"Send adorable Sunday in with more punch!" Edward yelled, and his friends thought he was absolutely hilarious.

"Don't *you* think she could model?" Mom asked Dad.

"I guess so. Should I go out and buy more ice cubes?"

"Maybe you could take more pictures, with the other camera, the Japanese one, and we could send them around to modeling agencies."

Edward's friends momentarily stopped trying to stomp on the balloons and play Frisbee with their paper plates. They took up the cry. "I want an adorable sundae with hot fudge and chopped nuts!" one of them yelled. "I bet I know what she'd be good at modeling—braces!" another one screamed. They sounded as if they were all going to die laughing.

Dad said he'd try to remember to pick up some film during the week, and he went out to the dining room to pour more punch and quiet down the little wimps.

Mom put my picture up on the kitchen bulletin board, and that's where it stayed for weeks, next to the one of Edward blowing out the candles.

* * *

The reason Dad didn't take pictures of me with the Japanese camera right away is because he travels a lot and was out of town practically for the rest of the month. When he did come home, he said he had no energy for anything but yawning, and that's what he did when he wasn't napping on the couch or asleep in his bed.

But the following weekend, Mom set aside Saturday morning for the photography session, and he posed me out on our back deck. Mom told me to wear something bright, then watched from the kitchen door and told me not to squint and to open my eyes wide and not to make that fake face I always make whenever I look into a camera. Edward remarked that if I could really make faces, I wouldn't have my own.

When the pictures came out, she spread them on the kitchen table and asked Dad to look them over.

I admit, the pictures looked not bad. In fact, I think I looked better in the pictures than I look in mirrors, because in the photographs you couldn't see the freckles, which I have not only across my nose but also on my forehead, and of course my teeth were now so straight they reminded me of the plaster replicas in the dentist's office he uses to show how to brush. Also, I had combed my hair, which is long, and that was the end of the summer, so it was lighter than usual. In August I am blonde from the sun, but by the time Christmas rolls around, I'm back to my normal borderline brown again.

Mom's hairdresser, Mr. Paul, who used to be a child star in Hollywood and appeared in three real movies that are still being shown on TV, looked over the photographs and said I definitely had the *makings*, and he told her to have three enlarged and send them right out to a talent agent without wasting a minute. He said he would find out who the best agents were because he had *connections*. He was sure nobody would turn me down.

Dad helped Mom pick out the three best poses, and Mom sent the enlargements out practically the next day. As Paul predicted, the agent didn't turn me down; on the other hand, he never answered Mom's note, either. We never saw those pictures again.

Then, a few weeks later, Mom met someone else who had connections, and she sent off more enlargements, this time with a long letter. She and I worked over that letter a whole evening because Mom wanted to make sure she put in every last thing I was good at, but the things that I am good at—math and baking meringue cookies and predicting weather—would not exactly put me on the cover of *Newsweek*, either.

When I was four, Mom had signed me up for ballet, because when she was a kid she used to be a fantastic figure ice skater. She used to wear a little fur hat with a matching little fur muff and those fur blobs on her skates and have her pictures in all the newspapers. She thought I could do that, too, but our town has no ice rink. Ballet seemed just as good, or even better, but after about a year and a half, it was obvious I was not going to move gracefully enough to warrant the big check Dad was writing to Miss Ellingarten's School of Dance every month. After seeing one recital, Dad said the money would better be invested in a new hot water heater, and even Mom had to agree that I was not cut out to be a ballerina. As for singing, no one even suggested lessons. When I sing, I sound like the garage door when it needs oil.

So Mom started the letter something like this:

Sunday is outgoing and friendly and loves animals. She is a good student and will be able to memorize lines well if asked to do television commercials. Last year, she won a blue ribbon for backstroke in the town swim meet and got an honorable mention in the diving competition. She can ride a bicycle and has studied ballet. . . .

"Mom!" I protested. "If they ever see the way I dance . . ."

"You can follow a choreographer perfectly well, dear," Mom continued. "Is there anything else at all you do that you can think of?"

"When I was in nursery school, we used to lie on mats after lunch, and I got an award for being the best rester, remember?" Of course, I meant that as a joke, but believe it or not, Mom added, "Sunday is patient and able to wait quietly for long periods of time, if necessary."

"I was picked best bubble-gum blower of the fifth grade," I reminisced. Not exactly star skills, but I still do blow the biggest bubbles in Stanhope, if not in the whole state of Connecticut.

So that went into the letter, too, along with my height, weight, and the fact that I can do cartwheels.

When the letter was all done, Mom looked pretty pleased with herself, and then she put down her pen and reached for an envelope big enough for the letter and the pictures, but suddenly, just before she stuffed the letter in, she stopped and looked at me.

"You know, Sunday, all this time I never asked you if *you* really wanted to do this—to model and maybe be on television. Do you?"

I didn't have to think about that more than a minute. Being on television seemed like the most exciting and glamorous thing that could ever happen to me, and imagine! I would actually be paid real money for having fun doing it. Not only that, but Mom explained that I might even have to miss school a day here and a day there.

Would I mind that? Do dogs have fleas? I wouldn't mind it, I told Mom.

And did I realize that I might not get every part I tried out for? Would I feel too awful and rejected if I was turned down?

I said I was pretty sure I could handle it. Wasn't I turned down for all-star soccer last year? That was terrible, but it only hurt for a few days. This couldn't possibly be worse.

Mom licked the envelope and sealed it. "I never want to

push you into anything, like those awful stage mothers who make nervous wrecks out of their kids. If it stops being fun, we'll stop it right away, okay?"

"Okay," I said, and that night I dreamed I got the starring part in a situation comedy about a girl who makes it onto the all-star soccer team. In my dream I was famous and rich and people asked me to sign their menus in restaurants.

How could anything that exciting ever stop being fun?

2

AS I said, I can predict weather better than the computers Dad sells for Consolidated Data Products. I think it's a skill I inherited from my Grandma Donaldson in Arizona, who has a knee that hurts whenever it's going to rain. My knee doesn't hurt, but ever since I fell out of a tree-swing when I was in first grade, my collarbone gets twinges before a rainstorm and really aches if there's going to be a thunderstorm or blizzard. Nobody in our house listens to the weather forecast on television anymore because my predictions are about a hundred percent more accurate, and on the nights Dad is home, he almost always asks me whether it's going to be raincoat and umbrella weather or whether it's going to turn cold. (If it's going to turn cold, my collarbone sort of just feels creaky.)

Weather is one thing, but who could have predicted

that not a week later we'd get a reply to Mom's letter from Mr. Farley, of Farley's Talent Agency, and that he wanted to meet me *as soon as possible*?

This time it was my mother who asked me what the weather was going to be like for my interview, so we could plan my wardrobe for the Big Day. It was all set for four-thirty, which would mean I wouldn't have to miss school and Madame Popindreau's verb and vocabulary test (my mother's idea, not mine), and we'd rush right down to the agent's office from school. Tomorrow!

The train would get us into the middle of the city in one hour and seventeen minutes, but then we'd have to take a taxi or a bus, and my mother was worried we'd be late, so she decided she'd drive in in our red Toyota, as long as I'd promised a sunny day so she wouldn't have to drive in the rain.

We also picked out a sunny-day outfit, which took about half an hour of what-goes-with-what conversation and looking through the clean and dirty laundry piles for my missing red-and-white striped blouse. (Whatever I want to wear is always missing.) It was in the back of my closet, with the blue corduroy pants my mother thought fit me just right, and the red belt that ties in knots. I thought I looked too patriotic, but my mother thought I'd struck the right balance of being well-dressed without being too-well-dressed. Whatever that means.

❖ ❖ ❖

I was dead right about the weather, as usual—blue skies, sunny, and warmish—but I could tell she was nervous anyway, because she kept talking about *my* trying not to be nervous, not fidgeting, and what had I had for lunch? She hoped it wasn't a meatball wedge, because there's so much garlic in school meatballs that it might make my breath smell and knock the agent out of his chair.

I told her I'd eaten the hamburger special and said I wasn't nervous, but I really was feeling tense enough to pull at the knots in my belt. I tried to picture the agent, but in my mind's eye all I could see was the face of Mr. Cartucci, my science teacher, who is so mean they call him The Whip. One look from him and you feel as if you've been lashed.

Thank heavens, the agent turned out to be absolutely nothing like The Whip. I played with my belt knots in the waiting room, sitting next to my mother and trying to read one of the old magazines lying on a coffee table there. I pretended not to notice the kid who had come in sometime before me and looked unbelievably bored, as if this was something she did every day of the week. Maybe she did; she looked just the way I wanted to look— with hair that wasn't borderline anything, but wisped around her ears and ran down her back in real golden-sunshine ripples—and skin on which no freckle had ever dared to show up.

She looked at me only for a second before they called her in, and fifteen minutes later she came out smiling. Her mother said, "How'd it go?" very softly, and the kid shrugged her shoulders in a way that said, of course it had gone well, why even bother to ask? She and her mother buttoned their jackets and left, looking as if a Rolls Royce was really waiting for them downstairs.

Mom dug into her purse and found a breath-mint candy and pushed it into my hand.

When the door opened, I practically jumped. A young man wearing a bow tie came out and handed my mother a yellow card to fill out, and he smiled at me. "We'll be calling you in in about fifteen minutes for a video test, so while your mother fills in the card, maybe you'd like to memorize these lines?" He handed me a slip of paper and I tried to play it very cool the same way the girl who'd gone before me had, but even grabbing my belt knots wasn't getting me calm. Lines to memorize! I squeaked out a "Thank you" and sort of wished we'd never started the whole thing and chewed down on my breath mint for courage.

I looked at the slip of paper and my mother read it over my shoulder:

"When my grandmother makes chocolate chip cookies, we all line up for a handful. They're the best, but—guess what! I just found out she always uses Sweet Tooth cookie mix! She fooled us all! Wow! Wait till I tell Daddy!"

While my mother wrote in my name and age and height

14

on the yellow card and added that I can blow big bubble-gum bubbles and dive off a high board, I read those lines over a hundred times. I tried not to move my mouth so that the nine-year-old kid in overalls who'd just come into the office with his mother wouldn't see me making a fool of myself.

Finally, after still two more kids had appeared in the waiting room with their mothers, the young man with the bow tie came back. "Sunday? You can come in now."

My mother started to get up, too, but the young man said, "Mr. Farley prefers to have a word with the child alone first," and Mom sank right down again. As I got up to follow him, she reached up and brushed a piece of hair off my forehead and wished me good luck. You would have thought I was going in for brain surgery.

I followed Bow Tie to a desk in an inner office that had walls covered with photographs of kids. It looked like kid-face wallpaper you could buy in rolls, and I recognized at least five of those faces, including Cousin Mindy. I've seen Cousin Mindy eat at least four thousand bowls of Little Farms Oatmeal "with honeyed apple bits and that reeeaal down-home flavor," and it seemed as if her face and all the other zillions smiling out from the walls were perfect, every single one without chipped teeth, big noses, or freckles.

The man behind the desk was bald and reminded me of my Uncle Walter except that he had a face as pink as a baby aspirin and the sort of little glasses you look over.

He had been looking at my photos on his desk, and now he looked over his tiny glasses at me. "So you're Sunday, eh? That's a great name! No one's going to forget a name like that, huh?"

I said I guessed not.

"So tell me something, Sunday. What's the thing you like best about school?"

I'd expected him to ask about the bubble gum or the ballet or the cartwheels, maybe ask me to open a box of gum and tell me to perform or something. Now it sounded as if he just wanted to chat. I relaxed a little. "I like gym when we have swimming or volleyball, I like meeting my friends in the cafeteria, and I like math pretty well. Even algebra."

"No kidding. I used to like algebra in school, too. What a coincidence! Now tell me what you hate most about school."

That was easy. The Whip. If your assignment was a minute late, or you tried to leave his class to go for a drink of water, or you were late for his class—watch out. I told Mr. Farley the whole thing, and he really seemed very interested.

Then he asked whether it was my idea to try doing commercials or whether it was my mom and dad's. I told him it was really Mom's idea.

His eyebrows went up over his little glasses. "Will you be missing any after-school activities you'd rather not give up?"

I knew he was making sure no one was trying to twist my arm to get me to work, and I assured him I liked the whole idea.

"In that case," he said, "we're going to give you a video-tape test." He called the young man back on a desk inter-com. "Have you looked over the script Fritz gave you?" I nodded. The relaxation went and I grabbed my belt knot again. A video test, and I'd forgotten half the script I thought I'd memorized!

But Fritz put me at ease and told me not to worry if I couldn't remember the whole thing, and Mr. Farley shook my hand and said he'd enjoyed our chat. "Don't worry, you'll do fine," he said, and he pulled off his glasses and winked.

I wasn't sure. Fritz led me into a room about the size and shape of the wardrobe closets in our old elementary school. It was windowless and painted light blue, and at one end there was an empty high stool, like the kind my mother uses to reach high things in our kitchen. Pointing at the stool was the video camera, and hanging over it were a bunch of bright lights.

"So you're Sunday, huh?" Fritz said, fiddling with the camera. "I used to know a kid called April, and you know, she was born in September!"

"Oh, really?" I kept trying to take quick glimpses of the little script while Fritz pulled the camera up and down and wrote things on the yellow card my mother had given back to him.

"Okay now, Sunday," he said, and he got very business-like.

He came over and pinned a microphone to my red-and-white shirt and told me to seem happy. Seeming happy is harder than being happy, which is what I would be as soon as this test was over, but I tried to work up a cheery face, looked up the way Fritz told me to, and when he said, "Okay, go!" I began to recite the script he'd given me.

Only of course, with that bullet-microphone right under my chin and the lights and the camera, after I'd said the first phrase, "When my grandmother makes chocolate chip cookies," the rest of the script flew right out of my head.

I grappled for the paper in my lap and began to read, "We all line up for a handful." I knew, even as I was reading, that not only did I not sound like Judy Garland or Shirley Temple, I sounded like a person with a reading disability who has also left her glasses in another room.

He let me go through the whole thing. Believe it or not, I even said *Sweet Thooth*, instead of *Sweet Tooth*, and then sort of giggled like a fool and tried it again. Then, after I'd said it right, I lost my place and sat there like I had turned as stiff as one of the legs of the stool, around which I suddenly realized I was now trying to wrap my legs.

So much for a career in the television world, and good-bye to fame and success. I could hear Edward jumping up the minute Dad came home saying, "She blew it!" And I could see Mom's face when the agent came out and tore up the yellow card, threw it in one of the waiting-room ashtrays, and set fire to it with a torch.

But a minute later, Fritz saved my life. "We're going to do it again, now that you've relaxed a bit. And, Heather, bring the energy level up, okay?"

"Sunday," I said, smiling. For a name nobody would forget, Mr. Farley's own assistant had forgotten it real quick.

"Oh, sorry! The last girl was Heather. I do see a lot of kids. Okay. Remember the energy level. And try to look at the camera as much as you can. Don't be nervous. Think of this as fun."

I did it again. It wasn't perfect, but I'll say this—it was quite an improvement. *Sweet Tooth* came out *Sweet Tooth*, and I looked up at the camera, and I even smiled once. Yes, it was fun.

Then Fritz shook my hand, told me I did well, made some more marks on my card and asked me if there was anything else about me he should know.

"Yes," I said. "I've made Sweet Tooth cookies, too. I brought some over to my friend Karen when she had the chicken pox about a month ago. And they *are* the greatest!"

Mom practically leaped out of her chair when I came back out of the office. She didn't have to ask me how it went because her *face* asked me how it went. "I think I was all right," I whispered, and Fritz asked her to come in to speak to Mr. Farley for a moment. I flopped into the leather couch next to the potted plant and sighed with relief. Wow. The ordeal was behind me, and Mr. Farley was going to sign me up.

I couldn't wait to tell the kids at school.

3

WHY didn't you tell me I'd be fogged in in Bangor?"
Dad asked when he called from Maine that night
to get the news.

I was still so keyed up, I kept laughing at everything
he said, even the stuff that wasn't funny—that he'd been
hoping to break open a bottle of champagne tonight to
celebrate my becoming a "real, live professional," and
that he'd gotten a good deal on a piston pump for which
he expected a thank-you note not only from Edward but
also from his fish, and now here he was, stuck in a motel
room in Maine watching other people's kids in TV commercials!

I told him my version of the day's events, and then he
and Mom talked for about twenty minutes about what
Mr. Farley had told her: that I might go out on lots of
auditions and never get a job, that we should never be

21

late or miss a scheduled appointment, that she'd have to give up a lot of her own free time to get me here and there, that we'd better think about buying a telephone answering machine so we could be reached at all times, and that we should have professional photographs taken for a composite right away.

All the time they were talking I could see myself holding up that box of Sweet Tooth Cookie Mix and convincing the whole United States of America to run out and buy cases of it. And most important, I could see my friends at school practically breaking into applause when I walked into Home Room.

Which is not exactly the way things happened. The next day Karen was really excited and wanted to hear every word of my adventure at the Farley Agency in New York, but the other kids lost interest fast because five minutes after I walked into Home Room, the principal, Mrs. Bealey, made an announcement on the intercom that was bigger news. This year the entire student body was to go on an end-of-year moonlight sail in a big boat up the Long Island Sound. The school intended to rent a yacht and hire a band and celebrate our eighth-grade graduation with a party we'd never forget.

The hitch was, we'd all have to help defray expenses by selling liquid soap, Florida oranges, or offering services like a car wash or lawn-raking for the rest of the year.

Of course, my first thought was that I didn't want to miss any of this, and right away I wondered if there might be a work conflict if Sweet Tooth or anyone else decided I had to audition on any given day, but I immediately put the thought out of my head. Commercials are not usually filmed on weekends, and auditions are held strictly Monday to Friday. As for doing my share, not only could I work Saturdays and Sundays for the school, but I was pretty good at washing Dad's car, so I immediately put my name on the Car Wash list.

Right under Stewart Bifield's.

It is my deep, dark secret that I've liked Stewart since sixth grade and that working on washing cars with him would not be like working at all, but more like an Awesome Opportunity. Awesome is the word everyone uses this year, and it really applies to Stewart. His eyes are the color of jeans after they've been washed ten times, and he always says, "How're you doin'?" instead of "Hello," and this year his voice got real low, and he has a way of looking at people out of the corner of his eyes instead of direct. He is also shy, but when he does talk, it is not only about baseball and hockey.

Sometimes it is about track. I asked him how fast he was running the mile these days when I ran into him after The Whip's class.

"About five minutes."

"Awesome!"

"Oh, well," Stewart said.

"Hey, I couldn't help noticing we both signed up for the car wash for the anniversary sail," I threw in.

"How about that."

"So we start the Saturday after next, isn't that right?" I knew darned well, but I wanted to keep the conversational ball rolling.

"Yah," said Stewart.

"I guess that won't be in conflict with my new career." Oh, why had I said that? Bragging my head off just because Mr. Farley put my name in his files? I guess I just wanted Stewart to know I was on the verge of Making It Big and Being Famous. Maybe.

"What career?" he asked, taking the bait.

"I may do TV commercials. I'm signed with an agent."

His eyebrows went up over his faded blue-jean eyes.

"Hey. Cool."

"But I don't think that should interfere with the car wash. We usually don't film on Saturdays."

"No kidding."

"Right. So maybe we could team up? Like, it might be faster." I didn't want to be pushy, but with Stewart, he sort of pushes you into being pushy.

"Why not," Stewart said, and his voice sounded lower than the baritone's in the school choir. "Well, I gotta run. Softball practice. I'm pitching."

Looking back on it now, I think I was pretty obnoxious that week, trying to push TV commercials, Mr. Farley, or Sweet Tooth Cookie Mix into every conversation. The kids were pretty nice at first, but finally they just looked

24

at me with a yawn written all over their faces. At home, even Mom got tired of listening to my new habit of scrutinizing the other kids I saw on television. As for Edward, he was in heaven with his new piston pump. For some reason, he thought the fish were going to jump out of the tank and shake his hand for being a good fish-nanny. "You're looking pretty happy there, Florence," he said to one of his finny little Black Tetras. "Feeling good, huh, Scamp?" he said to his favorite, a Silver Hatchetfish.

"Are you waiting for an answer?" I asked him.

"You don't understand fish," Edward said.

"Wrong. Fish are easy. It's you I don't understand."

Another thing I didn't understand was why no calls came from the Farley Agency. Even after the photographer sent us proofs, and Mr. Farley picked out five poses for the composite (me smiling, me laughing, me in profile, me serious, me with hair pulled up), and after I'd told everybody in school who'd listen that I was now Signed Up and Ready, nobody seemed to want me.

"So when is your face going to light up channel four?" Bim Haskelovanovitch turned to ask me in science. Bim has the distinction of being the only kid in school with sixteen letters in his last name, which he seems to think is quite an accomplishment; it's gone right to his head.

"By the turn of the century," I said, and I could see The Whip looking in my direction.

"Which century?" Bim asked.

"How many you gonna be around for?"

"Donaldson!" The Whip's voice slashed in my direction. "Silence is golden!" But then he added, "Your lab report was A-One. Don't spoil your image."

"Maybe you can read your lab report on channel four," Bim snickered under his breath.

He was not untypical. My image was slipping, not only in The Whip's class, but also among my friends, which is why I tended to be a little edgy these days.

Mom noticed it, but then she seemed a little jumpy, too, especially when the telephone rang. She was also very careful to leave the new answering machine on when we were all out and to check it the minute we came in.

"Don't be impatient," she said. "Nothing happens overnight."

"Except sleep!" Edward whooped. It seemed to me that lately he was not exactly tuned into my problems, but later, just before he went to bed, he said, "Don't worry, Adorable, they'll call. If they don't, they've got the brains of . . . ," he hesitated, looking for the right word.

"Your sardines," I said.

We got the call the day before the first Car Wash Saturday, and it figures. Good things always seem to come in batches, like Sweet Tooth cookies.

On the way out of school Friday, I reminded Stewart that I'd meet him at the Yellowbird Mobil Garage at ten o'clock to begin getting ready for the first car-wash customer, due any time after ten-thirty. He floored me by saying he'd come by my house, and we could bike over together at about quarter to.

Then he said, "What if it rains?" and I said, "It's not going to rain," and he said, "How do you know?"

"My collarbone isn't twinging." And he said, "Hey, cool," and I said, "No, warm," and he threw a wadded-up piece of paper into a trash can that was like a half a block away. He always practices throwing things and always gets a perfect hit. "You really predict weather?" I said "Yes," and he sort of gave a low laugh and looked at me out of the corners of his eyes and said, "Hey! Awesome."

An event like an Arrangement With Stewart doesn't happen every day, so I rushed into the house and was about to reach for the telephone to see if Karen had gotten home yet, when my mother came downstairs looking absolutely wired up.

"Mr. Farley's secretary called," she said, pulling out the words as if she was trying to make them last longer, "and we have our first commercial audition scheduled for Monday afternoon at two o'clock!"

I honestly thought she was going to spin right off the last step.

"So, aren't you going to say something?" she asked, when she saw my jaw just hanging open as if it were hinged.

"A commercial for what? What for? For what?"

27

"It's just to sit in the back seat of a car. It's for some new kind of radial tire. They want a ten- to thirteen-year-old character child."

I discovered that on television there are two types of kids: Beautiful Kids and Character Kids. Obviously, Beautiful Kids don't have freckles or noses the length of my nose, so I am classified as a Character Child.

"I can't believe it," I said. First Stewart, then radial tires.

"I can't believe it, either," Edward said. "Although I knew it would happen. Didn't I tell you it would happen?"

"You did."

I made a mental note to buy Edward a chocolate-covered banana and to stop riding him about his fish.

"Remember, you may not get the part, dear. Please, don't get your hopes all up," Mom said.

"They're already up. Too late," Edward said.

4

I T turned out that Stewart and I like the same radio station. He brought a portable along so we could work to music, and it was a great idea. We even pedaled across town to "Let's Hear That Beat" and "Dewy Eyes." Time really flew despite the work, and despite the fact that Bim Haskelovanovitch and his partner, Hiroshi Yamashita, were at work right near us. Hiroshi's English is not perfected yet, but he laughs whether he gets it or not.

"Didn't I see your face on the cover of *TV Guide*?" is the way Bim greeted me when Stewart and I arrived. Hiroshi laughed. It is to my credit that I didn't toss either a sponge or a bucket of water at him. I stayed absolutely cool.

"I'm going for an audition Monday for a radial-tire spot," I said, and then immediately regretted it, because if I didn't get a place in the back of that car and that tire commercial appeared on television with another Character Child in the back seat, Bim would never let me live it down.

"So, you gonna practice changing a couple radial tires here today?" Bim asked. Hiroshi laughed.

"Very funny," I said.

Maybe Mom was worried that my career was going to suffer because of dishpan hands; she had given me a pair of her old rubber gloves to wear. Bim, seeing the gloves, was really amused. "Gonna do a little surgery, too? Gonna be a very full day for you, huh?"

I looked at Stewart, who was not paying too much attention, thank heavens. He was fixing the antenna on his radio so we would get the best reception, and now he left to fill up a bucket with Liquid Dynamo and water. We were going to do a real razzle-dazzle job, he'd said. He said he wanted our cars to be the cleanest and the shiniest. Stewart likes competition.

Bim said, "Why are you tuned to that station? It's the pits!"

"The pits," Hiroshi echoed, nodding agreeably. Here was a word he had, obviously, quickly picked up.

"It's going to be very distracting," Bim added.

"Don't look at it," I suggested.

"The pits," Hiroshi said, and he winked, as if he'd invented the word himself.

Karen had just arrived. She waved to me from the other side of the lot. She and I would have teamed up if it weren't for Stewart, but that's what's nice about Karen: she's flexible. She'd asked Erin Wurtzel, the new girl, and felt she was doing a good deed in the bargain because Erin didn't know too many of the kids.

As soon as Stewart came back with the Liquid Dynamo and the pail of water, the first car pulled up, and we went to work. Stewart was terrific at organization, and he divided the job so that sometimes I did the fenders and windshields and he did the roof and the tires, or sometimes I vacuumed the inside and he waxed. It worked beautifully because we didn't have to talk the whole day (Stewart is not that much with words, except those that go with music, which he sort of sang along to once in a while), and because there were hardly any lulls. During lulls, Stewart practiced pitching the sponge into the pail. Cars came all day until four-thirty, when we quit for the day. The only other break was a quick lunch, which Stewart bought at Guacamole Joe's, across the road. (I reimbursed him although he did offer to pay.) We ate, sitting together on a low stone wall at the side of the gas station.

Even Bim didn't call over, except once or twice, to find out how much we'd made so far and to ask if my gloves were chapped. Hiroshi waved once, when we were both working on a Nissan sportscar. "Some car, yes? Japanese car!"

At the end of the day we finally tallied up the profits, and it was incredible that, even after subtracting for the

31

Liquid Dynamo and the sponges and wax we'd bought, Stewart and I had made almost seventy-four dollars!

I hoped Stewart would bike home with me, too, but he said he had to stop at the sporting-goods store and look over their new shipment of cleats before it closed. He said, "See ya around," and waved good-bye.

I couldn't say that I knew him any better than when we'd started that morning, but I did feel that we'd worked well together, and even if we didn't exactly have all the same interests, at least we both like Amos and the What-nots, the Crime Stompers, and the Heartfelt Four.

I called Karen the minute I hit home, and she told me Erin had turned out to be pretty neat but talked a lot about the two framed Beatles autographs she had hanging in her room and her collection of tennis trophies. Karen asked how it went with Stewart.

She knows I like him, but she knows how to keep her mouth shut, another good thing about her. She said she'd do her spy bit to find out if Stewart thought I was a good car-wash and biking companion, and what he thought of me in general.

The best thing about Karen is that she's not a bit jealous, and when I told her I was actually going to an audition Monday, and would get out of school early enough to miss French and gym, as well as science, she said, "Lucky duck" three or four times, and really meant it when she said, "I just know you'll get the part!"

* * *

Mom wasn't so sure I'd get it: on the way to the city in the car, she gave me a big lecture on why I might be rejected if I were going to be rejected. "Sometimes they think you're too old looking, or too tall or short, and it has nothing to do with your abilities. They might just pick a kid because she could be the brother or sister of another one of the kids they're considering."

I promised Mom I wouldn't go into a blue funk if I didn't get the part, and she said, "You are a sensible girl," and she gave me a breath mint. Then she wondered if it had been smart to wear the same overalls to the audition that I'd worn and crumpled around in at school all day. She also thought I could have washed my hair in the morning the way I had before Stewart was due Saturday. Then she told me please to remember not to slouch.

To be honest, by the time we got to East Ninth Street, she had me plenty keyed up.

The scene inside was not relaxing, either. I imagined there would be a few people waiting, the way there had been at the Farley Agency, but this seemed like a railroad station at rush hour—people milling around, lots of kids my age, as well as a bunch of younger ones (some of them seemed to know each other), mothers, a man in suspenders handing out cards and forms to fill out—a general hubbub.

Some kids seemed to have scripts to memorize, and some didn't. There weren't exactly enough to go around, but Mom finally got hold of one, and it turned out they'd called me because they needed some kids who could blow bubble gum. The commercial had to do with a family going out riding in this car with the new radial tires and the mother telling the father how safe and comfortable and pleasant the ride was, and all the while the three kids were cutting up in the back seat. The only line I'd have in the commercial would be, "Hey, it's my turn to sit next to the window!"

I don't think we were there more than ten or fifteen minutes when the same girl we'd seen at the Farley Agency, Heather, with the flowing blonde hair, arrived with her mother. In the midst of all the commotion, doors opening, people coming in and out, other people being called, kids and mothers signing names in the big ledger at the door, this kid stayed absolutely cool. Her mother showed her a script she'd borrowed from another girl, and she glanced at it once. She sat in one corner of a leather couch overflowing with other noisy kids, opened a book and began to read as if she were alone in the public library. Was she a Character Child? If she was, she was a Beautiful Character Child, and if I was going to be in competition with her, forget it—I'd never get the job!

Her arrival took my mind off the script, but not for more than a minute. I was back to, "Hey, it's my turn to sit next to the window," and in my head I must have said it four hundred different ways.

Finally a man in shirt-sleeves came out and called three names. Mine was one of them. Mom, who has been standing with another mother (her kid was a boy with almost-white hair), squeezed my arm in sort of a *bon voyage* squeeze, and in I went.

We were led into a big room, pretty bare, with lights, a video camera, more people milling around, and in one corner, a sort of low bench, which was supposed to represent the back seat of a car.

"So, you're Sunday Donaldson?" a lady said to me, and she wrote something on a clipboard she was holding in her hand. She seemed young and friendly. "Nice change after all the Jennifers I've seen today!"

She handed me a package of bubble gum and asked me to start chewing. Then she introduced me to Todd Something and Larry Something, who were supposed to be my brothers in this commercial, and she asked us to sit together on the bench. I sat in the middle and was supposed to look a bit put-out and say my line, "Hey, it's my turn to sit next to the window!" in sort of an annoyed tone.

Larry's line was, "She always gets to sit next to the window," and Todd, who looked about three, but was really almost six, said, "I want to thit on the roof." Todd looked even more nervous than I felt.

The lady told me to blow a bubble, the biggest I could, and look "a little pouty."

The red light on the camera meant that we were being videotaped, but I thought of it as a red, unclosing eye that was staring right at me, daring me to get that pink bubble bigger than a baby's head.

I didn't, of course, but I did manage to blow one Ping-

Pong ball size, pop it, say my line, and not fall off the bench. Todd messed up the first time and looked as if he were going to cry. We did it twice; the lady said, "Fine, kids, thank you very much," and that was it. She smiled, wrote something on her clipboard, and moved away. It was over. Somehow, I'd expected more. I guess I expected an instant verdict on whether I'd get to blow gum coast to coast or never again, and I now had no way of knowing whether I was in or out. Todd scrambled away fast and disappeared, and Larry said, "Thanks," and he took off after him.

"I think I did all right," I told Mom, but not until we were alone in the elevator together. I didn't want the whole waiting room to hear what I had to say. "At least I didn't goof anything up."

Mom was all smiles. "I'm sure you were darned good, Sunday," she said. "How about a little celebration? I saw a coffee shop on the corner. How would you like a soda?" Mom is not much for pushing sodas, so I knew she was in a good mood, and I was pretty thirsty and so relieved to have the audition behind me that it seemed a great idea.

So Mom and I slid into a booth and I ordered a Coke and a dish of ice cream, and Mom had a cup of coffee, and then she ordered a dish of ice cream, too. She had to think ice cream over for about five minutes first, though, because she said she can't afford to put on even one more pound. Did I realize she weighed only a hundred pounds when she and Dad were first married? she asked me. She is not fat or anything, but she certainly weighs more than a hundred pounds now. She then sort of got into talking about the way things were back then when she weighed twenty-five pounds less, and she'd get up every morning at five o'clock to practice her double axles and triple flips at the ice rink in Lapham, New Jersey, where she and Dad lived when they were first married. She told me about the time she got an audition with the Ice Capades and got sick to her stomach the day she was supposed to go, and Dad thought it was because she was so nervous, but it turned out she was pregnant with me! She never did go for that audition, but she said she never regretted missing it for one minute, after I was born. She did say she tried to go to the Ice Capades every year for years after that, and she asked if I remembered the first time she took me (I did; I was about four) and how she cried when they played "Tales of the Vienna Woods," which was the music to which she had practiced for a month for her audition.

Our ice cream came then, and we got very busy eating, and finally, when we were almost done, Mom put down her spoon and said, "You know, when I looked at that composite photograph of you, it just hit me how much you look like I used to look. Not in every pose. In the serious one, though, you look just like I looked in my confirmation picture. I even used to have freckles."

"No kidding! How did you get rid of them?"

37

"That's one of the only nice things about getting older," Mom said, and she gave me a smile that sort of went down around the edges. "Mine just disappeared. Gone for good," she said, trying to work up the corners of her mouth.

"I can't wait for mine to go, too," I said.

Mom shook her head. "Don't wish them gone, Sunday. They'll fade off soon enough."

Ziggy Mitchell, Edward's baby-sitter, had fallen asleep right in front of "Towers of Dark," my favorite television soap opera, so I couldn't ask him if Evangeline had died of her shotgun wounds. Edward hadn't even glanced at the television set. He was afraid Cassie, one of his Danios, might be egg-laden, and had pulled up a chair in front of the tank to wait for the eggs to fall. He was sitting there like a zombie when we walked in, chewing on a bare stick that had once held a chocolate banana.

"Did you get the job?" he asked, but he hardly took his eye off Cassie, the pregnant fish.

"Won't know for three days," I said.

Mr. Farley had warned that if we didn't get a callback or notification within three or four days, we could assume someone else had gotten the part.

"I'll check back in seventy-two hours then," Edward said, and Mom went in to wake Ziggy.

"Don't forget," I said, between two yawns, but I don't think he even heard me.

5

NOT only did no call come within three days, but Cassie the fish laid what seemed like a thousand eggs and then ate them before Edward could get her out of the tank. "Cassie, you jerk!" Edward screamed at the tank. The fish crisis and his own eating kept him busy until Friday, when Dad came home and made him help rake leaves. That took his mind off Cassie and my radial tire commercial by making him wheeze and sneeze. He is not only allergic to animals, but also to autumn leaves, and Dad had to let him off the hook after about twenty minutes and go it alone.

While Dad raked and Edward sneezed, I studied for the science midterm, which wasn't easy (I don't think I'm ever going to understand electricity), and Mom kept eyeing the telephone. Talk about electricity, she never said a word, but whenever it rang, it seemed as if she got a little charge that sent her flying to answer it. Of course, by Friday, we both figured it was too late.

One of those telephone calls was for me from Karen, who was ready with her report about Stewart. "I asked him what he thought of you during assembly today," she said Thursday night.

"What did he say?"

"He said you were okay."

"That's it? That's all? Just okay?"

"Well, you know Stewart. He keeps his thoughts to himself."

"He does, doesn't he?"

Karen giggled. "Did you ever think maybe he's afraid of an idea shortage? Maybe he hasn't got too many to spare."

"No. He's just quiet."

"I've seen him scream down the gym during basketball games."

"Maybe if I get a part in a sneaker commercial, he'll like me more." I don't know why I was laughing; I was in no mood to be amused.

"No developments on the radial tires?" Karen asked very carefully.

"Not yet," I answered, and that's another great thing about her. She could tell it was a touchy subject, and she was so tactful she never asked me again.

I try never to ask much about things that bother her,

either, like her home situation, for example. When Karen's Mom and Dad split up, when we were in the sixth grade, she couldn't take it and had to go up to her grandmother's in Canada and stay for about six weeks. When she came back she was fine, and it was like old times, except sometimes she got very quiet when you didn't expect her to get quiet, and once she had to leave the room when we were watching "Towers of Dark" after school and Wendy's father walked out on Wendy's mother. I followed Karen into the kitchen and kept saying, "It's just a soap opera, it's not real," but Karen was sort of hanging over the sink, staring at the taps. If she was crying, I couldn't tell, but she had torn off some paper towels and crumpled them on the counter, and I don't think it's because she'd washed her hands.

Not only did I not get the radial tire spot, but I tried out for another commercial about a week later (for headache tablets), and I went to a go-see (that's where about two kids out of two zillion are picked to be in a magazine or a mail-order catalog modeling something), and nothing came of any of it. At the go-see I ran into Heather again, sort of passed her in the hall, and by this time, I almost felt I knew her. I said, "Hello," and she said, "Hi," not unpleasantly, but not really friendly either.

By now, all the kids in school had stopped asking about my career, even Bim. When he reminded me that another car wash was scheduled for the following Saturday, he never mentioned television at all. Then, on Friday, in science, he really surprised me. "You're not a bad car scrubber. With your rubber gloves and my muscle, we'd really make a cool pair. Donaldson and Haskelovanovitch! How about it, want to team up this time?"

Of course, I'd practically held my breath whenever I saw Stewart, hoping he'd ask me to be his partner again (I couldn't ask him the *second* time), and just that morning, he'd stopped me in the hall. "How're ya doin'!" he said. He was standing under the big portrait of *The Blue Boy* near the principal's office, and I suddenly thought I saw a strong resemblance, until he continued, "Y'got any extra notebook paper? I just ran out, and I got nothing to write on."

"Sure." I tried to keep it light as the foam on the top of the bucket of Liquid Dynamo, but the disappointment was running deep. I also tried to work the car wash into the conversation. "Going to rest up for Saturday?"

"Why, what's Saturday?"

"Second Car-Wash Day."

"Oh, yeah, I forgot. No. I promised this guy I'd go on a five-mile run with him."

"Oh."

"Yeah. Well. See ya around. Thanks for the paper, Sun."

"Welcome."

Then he sort of stopped for a minute, like he had an afterthought. "Hey, you know, you look nice today," he said, and there was this little spot of color that came up in his left cheek and his right cheek. Like *The Blue Boy*.

"Thank you." I guess my cheeks turned the same color, because I could feel the tingling under my eyes.

Wow.

However, speaking of tingling, I turned Bim down for the car wash. "It's going to rain. Probably all day. There's not going to be a car wash," I said on Friday.

"How do you know?"

I told him about my collarbone, and he laughed for about ten minutes.

"You'll see," I said, and of course, on Saturday morning, before I even pulled up the shade in my room, I heard the rain beating like crazy on the roof. It went on all day and seemed like some kind of a sign—when things start to go wrong, like rain on a roof, they don't seem to want to stop: Edward's fish, my career, Mom's Sunday dinner (a new recipe made with soybeans we tried to pretend we liked eating), and, on Sunday night, the usual call from Grandma in Arizona, except with a new twist—her arthritis was getting worse, and someone had tried to vandalize Grandpa's car. That put Dad in a worried mood, and he said now it looked as if he might have to fly down and visit his parents—they were getting old—although he didn't know when he was going to find the time; the company was working him to death as it was.

Then, on Monday, when I thought the grim streak was over, The Whip called me to his desk after class.

My knees felt as if they were bending the wrong way when I had to walk up the aisle after the bell rang.

"Okay, Donaldson," The Whip said, and he handed me my science test, with its big red 62 smack in the middle. "How come?"

I opened my mouth but nothing came out.

"Didn't you study for this exam?"

"Yes," I said.

"You don't seem to know too much about positive and negative charges."

I shook my head.

"You missed three different classes, all of them dealing with electricity. It's no wonder you didn't understand electrons and positrons." He had his little gray book and he was pointing into it with his silver pen. Whenever The Whip pointed that pen at a kid, I imagined it might turn into a sword that he might run right through a kid's heart.

He pointed it at me now. "This is not like you. If you need extra help, come after school this week. I'm here for extra help every Thursday. Okay?"

"Okay."

"Let's get back in shape, Donaldson!" The Whip said, putting the pen in his shirt pocket. "And start reading up on the aurora borealis."

"Yes, Mr. Cartucci," I said, and I was so glad to get out of there, I nearly flew to my next class.

Luckily, I am pretty good in French, so skipping a class now and then doesn't matter; when Madame Popindreau gave back our midterms a half-hour later, I had a neat 92 on my test paper, and I took that as sort of a good sign. Now maybe everything would turn itself around and good luck would start zapping me like positive and negative charges.

And sure enough, when I got home, there were other omens—Edward was out helping some kid with his paper route, so the house was really peaceful and quiet, Dad was coming home for dinner, and Mom was making my favorite dish, stuffed meatloaf, and she was humming.

Humming is the sure sign of good news; we'd had another audition call. This was an important commercial for Down Home Peanut Butter, and the date of our audition was the twelfth, at three o'clock.

"I've got a good feeling about this one," Mom said, and that just goes to show you that that old saying, "Mother knows best," can really be off the mark.

She was about as wrong as anyone could ever be about anything; here I thought good fortune was ready to smile on me at last, but that audition was such an awful experience, I was ready to quit the idea of doing commercials or modeling, or any kind of performing, forever. In fact, it made me feel so awful I wanted to crawl into my bed and stay under the covers until my freckles disappeared, my nose shrunk, and I got as old as my grandma in Arizona.

6

IF the radial tire tryouts seemed a hubbub, the waiting room of this casting studio was a madhouse. Wall-to-wall kids, mothers, a couple of grandmothers, a father or two, and the usual people with pads or clipboards running in and out. This time, somebody was smoking, although a big sign said, THANK YOU FOR NOT SMOKING. Nobody seemed to care, and the place was getting blue and hazy.

And there was little Todd, the kid who'd tried out with me a couple of weeks ago, with his mother, and off by herself as usual, Heather the Cool. She was top-to-toe in bright red today, and you couldn't miss her, although she was sitting in the far corner of the jammed waiting room, right under the storyboard, reading what looked like the same book she'd been reading every time I saw her. I'd brought my science textbook, but concentrating on the aurora borealis was not easy.

I went over to look at the storyboard, which was hanging almost over her head. The storyboard is a sort of description of the commercial, done by a cartoonist. It looks almost like a page cut out of a comic sheet, showing what's going to happen in the first scene, the second, the third, and so on.

Now I understood why there were so many kids here today; this Down Home Peanut Butter commercial was going to be filled with them—lined up on a football field and marching like a school band behind a bunch of cheerleaders, and followed by an English sheepdog mascot.

I was trying out to be one of the cheerleaders, and my only line was, "Spread with jelly or just plain, Down Home chunky wins again!"

It seemed easy enough, and I was really almost getting used to these tryouts; I was hardly nervous. In fact, I was feeling so calm and relaxed that since I was standing in front of her, I felt it would be unfriendly not to say hello to Heather the Cool again. "Hi."

She smiled, and although it wasn't one of your ear-to-ear variety, the grin did seem warmer than last time. "Hi," she said, and after a minute she asked me if I was trying out for one of the cheerleader parts.

"Yes," I said.

"I'm trying out for the drum majorette." Heather now seemed a lot less distant than I'd thought she was.

According to the storyboard, the drum majorette headed the march, wore one of those enormous, shiny high hats

47

with pompons and strutted in high boots twirling a baton. Awesome!

"Can you twirl a baton?" I asked. I had tried once, just once. It felt like I was waving a leg of lamb in the air.

"It's not that hard."

"Where did you learn to do it?" I asked.

"Talent Academy," Heather said.

Her mother added, "Heather learned tap and ballet and juggling and even how to ride a unicycle there, too. Have you studied at the Talent Academy?"

I hadn't even noticed Heather's mother, who had seemed to pop up from behind a table lamp. She was sitting sort of behind it and had to keep leaning forward to talk.

I told her I'd never heard of Talent Academy.

"Heather's been going since she was three years old."

"Wow," I said. I told her I'd first seen Heather at the Farley Agency and assumed Mr. Farley had just signed her up, and that she was new at this, the way I was. Heather's mother threw her head back and laughed as if she wanted the laugh to travel to the next building. "Mr. Farley is her third agent. She's been at this for *years*. Her father and I are both in show business. Her father leads a society orchestra, and I sometimes sing with his band. I used to have my own nightclub act."

"How great!" I sighed. Well, no wonder Heather seemed so calm; she was used to the life, had been brought up with it. Probably went to Hollywood for vacation every year.

"We're just a bunch of hams, I guess," Heather's mother said, and she reached over and patted Heather's bright red sleeve.

Heather asked if my mother or father were in show business, too. I told her about my mother's budding ice-skating career but explained that she had to retire long ago.

"Oh, how sad," Heather's mother said, and at that moment the door to the inner office opened and a tall man with a gray beard began reading names in a low and steady voice. The room quieted as if he'd shot a cannon through the blue smoke. Heather's name, which turned out to be Burstein, was called first, and mine second. Four more kids were called, all girls, and although we were all supposed to be about eleven years old, I'd just turned thirteen, two of the girls were really fourteen, Heather was thirteen and a half, and one of the girls was really fifteen!

We were led into a really large studio that looked like Miss Ellingarten's Dance Studio, and the gray-bearded man seemed to have a whole bunch of other friends who were going to help him decide which of us was in and which of us was out, including a lady wearing a sweat-shirt with a picture of a banana on it, two men in three-piece suits like the kind Dad usually wears to work, and two or three other people I didn't really get a good look at.

The lady in the banana sweatshirt began to give us directions. "Okay—everybody ready? You all feeling good?"

We all said Yeah or Fine or Okay.

"All riiiight! Then let's line up, girls!" she said, and she showed us spots on the floor where we were to stand, a couple of feet apart. It reminded me of squad lines in gym. Then, when we were in position, she did some marching steps forward and back, forward and to the side, then to the other side, and asked us to follow. "Like thiiiis!" she said, and she brought her knees up high and pointed her toes. "In rhythm now—one and two and three and four—girls, Joe is going to play a tape, and I want you to step in rhythm, okay?"

Easy enough. One and two and three and four. Back and forward and to the side and forward. A snap.

The music began and we all did it.

Then, "All riiiight, girls, once more, please!"

We marched. One and two and three and four. Simple!

Now the banana lady handed the baton to Heather, and Heather began spinning it in front of her for practice. I would have given anything to be able to twirl a baton the way she could, as if it were—yes—electric! It really looked as if it were running on a battery or propelled by electrons and positrons, whatever they were.

Then we tried it all together one more time, Heather in front, the rest of us marching behind.

"Dynamite!" the banana lady said.

I was feeling pretty good about not getting out of step and getting my knees "really up there!" and then the gray-bearded man switched off the music and asked us to say our line, all together first, then one at a time. "Give it life, kids!" he yelled. "Give it everything!"

And then the banana lady threw her arm up as if she were leading a four-hundred piece orchestra, and she yelled, "And smile! Smile if it *kills* you!"

We screamed it out. Loud and clear, twice. And I smiled until my mouth felt out of shape. "Really great!" She applauded.

Then they called our names, one at a time. The fifteen year old went first: she practically yelled the lines and smiled like crazy. "Fine, Stephanie!" the gray-bearded man said. He had a whispered conference with one of the men in the three-piece suits, and I heard him say, "Perfect. She's dynamite." Dynamite seemed to be the *in* word here.

Now it was my turn. I practically sang, "Spread with jelly! Or just plain! Down! Home! Chunky! Wins! Again!" And I smiled so hard I thought my face was going to crack.

Now Gray Beard and both of the men in the business suits went into a huddle about me. Was I dynamite, too?

I guess I'll never forget just how they looked and the

51

color of the shirt the bearded man was wearing. It was the same dark red as the mixture Mom makes me swallow when I have a night cough, and it tastes as if it's going to melt your tongue and tonsils down when you swallow it. I'll remember the shirt forever because it was part of that awful scene that I have played in my head I don't know how many times since it happened.

I saw one of the young men in the three-piece suits shrug and rub a spot right over his glasses, and then I heard the bearded man say, "Too awkward. And she's just not pretty enough. What agency sent her?"

I wasn't meant to hear it. I know I wasn't. The problem was that I heard it as clearly as if they'd screamed it over a public-address system. And what was even worse was that every other person in that room heard it. All the girls, including Heather, the banana lady, and the other people milling around, heard it. Maybe it was even loud enough to go through the walls and into the waiting room. No, it only seemed that way.

I could feel everybody's eyes swivel to my face to see if I'd caught it and how I was taking it. I could feel the silence in that room as if it were a combination of hail and rain and sleet nailing me into the floor.

Gray Beard had absolutely no idea that he'd made the terrible announcement to the world and that I would have felt less shot-down if he'd just emptied a revolver into my head. He thought he'd *whispered* it. "Fine, thank you, Sunday," he now said in a normal voice and wrote something in a little notebook with a pen that looked like a twin of The Whip's.

I don't remember how I got there, but I guess I slunked away into a corner and just sank down in an empty chair to recover. I knew if I walked out of the studio that minute, Mom would see my face and know some terrible thing had happened. I needed a couple of minutes to pull myself and my face back to normal.

I pretended I had to tie my shoelaces, so nobody else could see my mouth wobbling, either. I also suppose, judging by the heat that seemed to be rising up my neck, that I might have turned the color of the bearded man's shirt myself.

Then I felt someone next to me and saw bright red out of the corner of my eye. I didn't really want to look up, but I did, and there was Heather, who was crouching on the floor next to my chair. "Listen, Sunday, you can't pay attention to everything they say about you. If you do, you'll go loopy. You can't take it seriously."

"Oh, I know," I managed to say, and I tried to sound as pulled-together as she did, but I wasn't fooling anybody.

"It's part of the business," Heather said, and she offered me a tissue. "There's nothing wrong with you, there really isn't."

"Oh, it really didn't bother me, honestly." I took a tissue and blew my nose. "I guess I'm just allergic, like my brother. Must be a lot of dust in here," I said, and then they called "Burstein" and Heather ran off to twirl her baton and strut, and to look beautiful in red, real dynamite, in front of the next bunch trying out to be cheerleaders.

As soon as we got home, I headed right for my room. I wanted to figure out a way to tell everybody I wasn't cut out for show business, and I needed a while to think. I'd pulled off "everything went swell" on Mom, who had had a short chat with Heather's mother after I left the waiting room and had other things on her mind. "Maybe there's something like a Talent Academy in our area. Some of these kids are getting a real edge on you by having had all these lessons," she said on the way home.

I couldn't get myself to answer.

"Heather's mother said Heather can even ride a unicycle, and she's starting Heather on tap and disco dancing."

I said nothing.

"The problem is that it might be expensive. We're going to have to look into it."

"Mom, I'm so tired." Enough was enough. "I think while we drive, I'll just nap, okay?"

"Of course, darling. Go ahead. I should have realized you must be exhausted."

We ate what seemed like an ordinary dinner. Edward talked fish, Mom talked auditions and chicken-and-carrots and city traffic, and Dad talked about Grandma. He said he'd called her and she was feeling better, but Grandpa didn't sound one hundred percent. Grandpa had offered to send airplane tickets if we'd all come for Thanksgiving.

Mom thought that wouldn't be a bad idea, and I thought it would be great. I love going to visit my grandparents. Their house is filled with knicknacks and old magazines and creaks when you walk across the floor. Also, Grandpa lets me help with the books. He taught me how to add and subtract the figures in one of the big ledgers in his office. He sells factories and office buildings, and there are endless things to do and columns to add. It cheered me right up. In Arizona I didn't have to be pretty or sing or act or dance. I could just be a blob and enjoy myself.

Edward also liked the idea. Grandma bakes like crazy, so at the mention of Arizona, his eyes lit right up.

My appetite for carrots and chicken improved, and things seemed much brighter than they had a half-hour ago.

Even Dad seemed cheerier. "Come in the den and watch *Wellington* with me," he invited Edward and me after dinner. I didn't really want to watch a long movie about English history, but while Mom pushes healthy eating, Dad pushes learning, and it was hard to turn him down. Aside from educating us, he loves company when he watches television.

So Edward and Mom and I stuck the dishes into the

dishwasher real fast so we could all sit together and watch *Wellington*, and I got my second jolt of the day after about half an hour.

The movie was not that bad—there were bloody war scenes, and it turned out much better than I expected—and I was really sort of caught up in it. Then, as usual, right in the middle of an interesting battle at sea (a man's arm was knocked right off his body by a cannonball, and the fingers moved even after they were dead), the movie stopped and the commercials came on.

First, a mouthwash commercial, then an ad for a new horror movie, and then an announcer's face appeared, framed in a big black rubber radial tire, and he asked, "Have you ever asked yourself, 'How safe is my car on the road?' "

I froze, went absolutely stiff.

There, in the next scene, was Heather, in the back of a car, sitting between Todd and Larry, blowing a pink bubble the size of a Ping-Pong ball.

Mom made a sort of burble that sounded like she'd swallowed something without chewing, maybe something the size of a Ping-Pong ball, and Dad said, "What's the matter?"

Heather spoke her line, "It's *my* turn to sit next to the window," clearly and perfectly, and Edward, the King of Delayed Reaction, yelped, "Hey, isn't that the commercial Sunday tried out for?"

Mom shushed him and patted my knee.

"It's okay, it's okay." I swallowed hard. "Heather's good in the part, really good," I said as the announcer squeezed the tube around his head and explained why these tires were better at keeping loved ones safe on the highway than all other radial tires made today.

"Y'mean you lost out to that *creep*?" Edward yelled. "I don't get it. You could blow a bubble twice as big as that. I've seen ya do it!"

Dad told Edward he'd said enough.

Edward never thinks he's said enough. "Sunday would've been better, a thousand, million, hundred times better," he added.

Mom said, "By this time next year Sunday will be appearing on television every day of the week!"

"Thank you and forget it," I said, and as soon as I could do it, without looking like the Number-One Poor Sport of Connecticut, I excused myself and went to bed.

7

A S I said, in my life, when disasters happen, they happen in bunches:

The very next afternoon, The Whip handed out paper
without batting an eye and sprang a surprise quiz on the
aurora borealis, ten terrible questions I answered with
four answers and six blanks. Also, my collarbone twinged,
meaning the last car wash of the season was going to be
rained out tomorrow (good-bye to seeing Stewart), and
Bim Haskelovanovitch stopped me in the hall after science to ask what I thought of the quiz, wasn't it awe-
somely *easy*, and since I'd been right last time, could
I give him a weather report for the weekend?

And by the way, he'd happened to be watching *Wellington* last night, and this kid appeared in a radial tire
commercial, and how come it wasn't me? Was there going
to be another radial tire commercial with me in it?

I thought of a lot of excuses I could make up, and I even considered just walking away as if I hadn't heard the last question or dropping my books to divert the three or four kids who were standing around waiting for the answer, but I guess all those years of Sunday School have given me a conscience that never knows when to stop, and I told the truth. I said, "I just didn't get the part."

I suppose my admitting it really surprised Bim. "You didn't?" he asked, his face looking as if I'd revealed I'd never learned to tell time, or slept standing up in the garage.

"My friend Heather Burstein got it." Maybe "friend" was pushing things a bit, but my conscience seemed to allow it, although reminding me "new acquaintance" would have been more accurate.

"Wasn't she good?" I asked. I meant it, too.

"Oh, I don't know . . . ," Bim said. "You could probably have done pretty well."

"Much better!" Karen loyally chimed in. She had just run up from gym in time to hear the last few exchanges and to walk to French class with me. "I saw it, too, but I wasn't going to mention it. I didn't think the girl was that great in the part."

"Naw good," Hiroshi said. "The pits."

I went the whole rainy/cloudy weekend not having the nerve to tell Mom and Dad that I was quitting show business, and I don't know why. Dad didn't really care one way or another, and Mom would have understood, but I kept thinking that with only about ten days left before Thanksgiving, I'd hold out until we got back from Arizona. That way, if anyone was even slightly disappointed by my not sticking with it, at least I wouldn't ruin a perfectly good holiday.

Also, I'd have to tell Mom and Day why, and I didn't want them to know what had happened at the Down Home Peanut Butter tryouts. They would get pretty upset if they heard what Gray Beard said about me; I could practically see Mom's eyes get big as half-dollars and hear volcanoes erupt in Dad's voice.

The disasters continued on Monday afternoon. The sun glanced off The Whip's bald spot, and the light seemed to bounce right into my eyes when he cracked at me, loud and sharp, in front of the whole class. "Donaldson! Your quiz is here in my hand with a grade on it. I won't tell you what the grade is, but I'll give you a hint! It's less than the amount of fingers you have on your right hand." He paused for the class to hoot with amusement and stamp feet. "And unless you grew a couple of extra thumbs and pinkies since last week, you didn't pass!"

I went hot and cold.

"And didn't we agree you were to see me after school for extra help?"

Cold and hot.

"So where were you last Thursday?"

If Gray Beard had thought I was too awkward on Thursday, he should see me now. My mouth had stopped working, and I had to keep my hands in my lap to keep my knees from thumping against each other.

"It would be one thing if you weren't capable, but your first three test grades this term were very high. Your report on water power was one of the best in the class, and your notebook has been well-organized and neat. Now let's cut our losses, shall we, Donaldson?"

I shook my head yes, without knowing what cutting losses meant.

"Remember to read up on the aurora borealis for the final. And you have a report due on James Watt at the end of this month."

"Yes, sir." It took about five minutes for my knees to quiet down.

Was I glad to get out of school and get home? Yes, for about five minutes.

Edward was at the kitchen sink, cleaning out his tank filter. "Where's Mom?" I asked.

He had this goofy smile on his face, like he knew something I didn't. "Waiting for you upstairs. She bought you something at the drugstore. We stopped on the way home after she picked me up from school. I don't want to mess up the surprise, but it's something in a green package about this big. . . ."

He held his wet, drippy hands out to illustrate and let

61

the water splat off them onto the floor. I noticed some chocolate on his wrist and around his upper lip. Edward the King would be rolling in his royal grave if he could see his namesake now.

I imagined some little goodie like a chocolate turkey (Edward had eaten his) or a new set of barrettes. My hair had really grown pretty long since last year. Maybe one of those neat comb and mirror sets Karen just got from her father, or an ounce of Essence de Mer, my favorite perfume.

Wrong. This was still disaster week, and my mother's idea of a little surprise was a box of Bianca Beaumont Lemon Highliter.

"What's that?" I asked, when she unwrapped the package and plunked herself into the rocker in the corner of my room.

In a voice that was so normal she might have been talking about a new brand of mouthwash with germ-killing ingredients, she said, "Hair lightener. It's going to put more blonde highlights into your hair."

"Mom, you're kidding!"

"I'm not kidding, Sunday—it's a wonderful idea. Heather's mother uses it on Heather's hair every three weeks."

"Mom, you're not seriously thinking of bleaching my hair!"

"Not bleaching, honey. Just *lightening*. With all natural ingredients." She held up the box to show me where it said, "Nothing artificial. No harsh chemicals. No per-oxide!" And then she added, "We got a call today," and her eyes brightened up as if she'd given *them* a quick Bianca Beaumont rinse, "and it sounds like a really good opportunity. They're using a lot of kids for a commercial for Tough-and-Ready Sneakers. It's going to be filmed at a stable in Long Island, and they're going to be running the kids around a track—right behind the horses!"

I think I turned hot and cold again. I imagined me with fake blonde curls, running a track. I imagined Gray Beard looking at my crazy yellow hair, around my freckled not-pretty-enough face, my huge, awkward feet that might not fit into any Tough-and-Ready sneakers on the market, maybe even imagined another "Thank you very much, Sunday," another "Which agency sent *her*?" and I started to feel not-so-good.

Mom went right on holding the box up as if she were doing a commercial herself. "I wouldn't use just any old thing on your hair. It's got an excellent conditioner in it! I was going to take you to Mr. Paul and have him do it, but his prices are a bit high, and until you land that first job, this will do the trick. Heather's mother. . . ."

I knew that no matter what Heather's mother said or did, I wanted my own hair with its own boring, unlight-ened, unconditioned, dirty, nonblonde streaks. As hair goes, it's not that bad.

But I know Mom. I can never win an argument with her, and I knew better than to try. I said I'd think about it and that sort of satisfied her for the time being, although I think she'd intended to bleach me out then and there and would have run for a towel if I'd let her. I had a better maneuver I could use, and with it I knew I'd win.

I'd get Dad on my side.

The minute he got home.

I'd show him the box of Bianca Beaumont and tell him I didn't want to be a tinted or highlighted blonde. He'd agree with me—that was a sure thing.

The problem was, he didn't come home until pretty late that night, and he was tired and cranky to begin with. I should have known enough to wait until tomorrow, or better still, just hide the Highliter until it all blew over.

So, in a way, I got what I deserved.

While Mom was reheating the fish stew she kept saying would never taste as good as when it was fresh, I followed Dad into the living room. He sat at his desk in the corner and began opening the mail with his letter opener, and I said, "Dad, I don't want to get my hair lightened with Bianca Beaumont Highliter."

He was paying no attention to me whatsoever.

He just kept slicing open the letters and flipping the junk mail into the wastebasket.

"Dad—please talk to Mom."

"Honey. I'm reading my mail."

I guess I must have said it three times before he finally really looked up, pulled his glasses down his nose, and took it all in.

Then he threw down the letter opener, jumped up, and ran into the kitchen.

"Shirl, what's this about Sunday's hair?"

"It's not a bleach. And it washes out after about five or six shampoos," Mom said. "I thought we could try it!" Her voice got small and wavery.

She was at the stove stirring, and the clouds were coming up from the pot. The moisture made my collarbone ache even more than it was already aching, and the way Mom and Dad were looking at each other made my head ache, too.

"I don't like the idea—not a bit!" Dad said. "And there's not a thing wrong with Sun's hair. I like it just the way it is!"

Good old Dad. His hair is the same color as mine, what's left of it. I knew he'd be on my side, but I didn't realize he'd get angry. I hate it when my parents fight. When I was little, I'd run into my room, jump in bed, and cover my head with a pillow. I felt like doing that now.

Dad's voice was getting higher, and Mom was trying to calm him and make her point.

"Please, don't fight," I said. It was my fault for opening my mouth. Lucky Edward was asleep and missing it all. He hates to see Mom and Dad fight even more than I do.

"We're discussing, not fighting," Mom said, but she looked hurt and upset, and her fist was clenched around a wooden spoon.

"Throw the stuff away," Dad said. "Into the garbage!"

"I was only trying to give her every advantage . . . ," Mom defended. Her voice went up.

"If you don't throw it away, I will."

"Why don't you sit down and eat your dinner, Steve? It's ready."

Dad sat at the kitchen table and stared at his placemat.

"I don't know what got into you, Shirl, I really don't," he said. "She's not even fourteen years old!"

Mom put the fish stew in front of Dad, and he looked at it as if the fish were still alive and ready to bite him.

"I'm not very hungry," he said.

The next morning when I told Mom I felt too sick to go to school, let alone to the Tough-and-Ready audition, she came and sat on the edge of my bed and brought me a cup of tea and a glass of orange juice. I did feel plenty sick; I wasn't making it up, but I kept wondering if Mom believed me.

Then she said, "You know, Sunday, Dad was right. Your hair is fine the way it is, and I apologize. I got carried away. I felt so bad that you hadn't gotten any of the parts you tried out for that I wanted to help."

Why wait for after Thanksgiving? Now was the time to tell her that if they didn't want me, I didn't want them. I opened my mouth to tell Mom, but she went on, "You know, Sunday, you're terrific, the way you persevere. Not many girls would be such good sports about being rejected again and again. I've got to hand it to you, you're a real trouper. You don't just give up. Honey, I'm so proud of you!"

Mom put her hand on my forehead and said she thought I might be running a slight fever. She was going right to the phone to call off this afternoon's audition. Too bad about running around the race track; it would have been fun. "But there'll be others," she said, leaving my room. At the door she turned. "And we'll show them all!" She waved her arm in the air as if she were trying out for the part of a baton-twirler, too.

So I kept quiet, and I don't know why, but I suddenly remembered what the lady with the banana on her skirt had said to us at the peanut butter audition: "Smile if it *kills* you!"

And I tried, I really did.

8

THE funny thing was, I came home from my grand-parents' with hair almost as light as Heather's. I guess Bianca Beaumont doesn't sell much hair lightener in Arizona; the sun had bleached mine out better in one week than a whole summer's sunning at the beach in Connecticut. I even got a nice tan in the bargain—and hardly any new freckles. Both Grandma's knee and my collarbone had accurately predicted no rain, no mist, no cold, and it was an absolutely great week for everybody, even for Edward. He was nervous about leaving his fish in the care of Ziggy Mitchell because he was sure Ziggy was going to throw too much food into the wrong corner of the tank or forget to come three days in a row. He spent the night before we left saying good-bye to Cassie and Florence and Ted and on and on. He was worried that Scamp looked sick. "I don't think he feels well," he said about six times.

"Throw him an aspirin," I suggested.

We got along better in Arizona, though. We played Hearts with Grandma and Grandpa every night, and we both helped Grandma make cactus candy. She said it helped her get her mind off her arthritis, and it was so delicious Edward said he liked it even better than chocolate bananas.

It was great to be back in my grandparents' house and to check out all the stuff that's actually been lying around since I was too short to reach it. I never get tired of going through old magazines that were printed when Mom was my age and statuettes that glow in the dark and ashtrays shaped like hands and little china animals no bigger than stuffed olives. Grandma never throws anything away.

Arizona is great, too, even though Dad warned me not to go barefoot the day he and Edward and I played croquet in the backyard. "Watch out for black widow spiders and scorpions. Also, rattlesnakes."

"You're kidding," I said.

"Cross my heart," he said. "If you don't believe me, ask Uncle Walter."

My uncle, Dad's brother, lives near Grandma and Grandpa, and he came over for Thanksgiving dinner. He brought his kids, our cousins, three little kids who all look like Aunt Cheryl, from whom he just got divorced. I liked it better when she used to come, too, because Uncle Walter lets the kids run wild, and one of them almost broke an antique paperweight with three real four-leaf clovers frozen in glass and then cried for about an hour even though nobody yelled at him.

So we had a pretty noisy Thanksgiving dinner. I think the only time they were quiet was when they listened to Mom talk about my great new coming career on television. I just filled my mouth with stuffing and never said a word.

Just as I predicted, Grandpa took me to his office and let me work on his books, but we didn't stay all day like we used to. Grandpa gets tired more easily and likes to go home and take a nap after lunch. I could see he was walking slower, too.

One night after dinner, Dad and I hiked into town together, and we stopped at a corner variety store so Dad could get some suntan oil and an evening newspaper and I could buy picture postcards. On the way out he got so engrossed in a magazine that was lying on a counter near the door, he forgot he'd promised Mom a new paperback and me a can of cold soda. I went to the back of the store to pick one out of the cooler, and when I got back to Dad, he was still flipping the pages of this little magazine.

I looked to see what he was reading that could be that interesting. It was a real-estate brochure, full of Arizona houses, pages and pages of them.

"You buying one of those, Dad?" I asked, just kidding, and Dad flipped a few more pages and shrugged.

"Maybe some day, Sun," he said, and then he showed

me a photograph of a gorgeous, modern, sort of flat house with pillars and a tile roof built around a bright-blue swimming pool with a big saguaro in front. Saguaros are those great big cactus plants you see a lot on picture postcards in front of sunsets.

"Not bad, huh, Sun?" he asked, and he smiled.

"Not bad," I said, and he closed the magazine and put it down on a pile of others just like it.

Then, as soon as we were outside, he put his arm around my shoulders and told me to look up at the sky. Like Grandma collects knicknacks, Arizona must collect stars; there seemed to be double the number we had at home up there!

We didn't rush home but walked slowly together down these really neat, quiet, and flat streets, and although it was cool, I hardly needed a sweater. At home I'd be buttoned up to my chin in wool and scarves, and here we were, three days before Thanksgiving, wearing shorts and making plans to go swimming tomorrow.

"I love the Southwest, I always have," Dad said, and he breathed in the air as if he were just coming out of a submarine. "I can smell the stars here, I really can. Can't you?"

I took a deep breath and decided I could smell them, too.

That's what I wrote on my postcard to Karen. She wouldn't think my saying that I could smell things in the sky was crazy at all. She kept telling me how lucky I was to have gotten to go to Arizona and to eat turkey for Thanksgiving; her dad was taking her and her brother to a Japanese restaurant because his girlfriend was a vegetarian. I also wrote, "I am bringing you some of Grandma's cactus candy. You'll love it," to cheer her up.

To Stewart I wrote, "I am really resting up for the Christmas tree ornament sale in December and the orange-grapefruit sale in January." Those were the fund-raising events scheduled until the weather permitted car washes again in the spring. I also wrote, "Will see you soon," and hoped he'd pick up the hint before the basketball season hit.

I even wrote a card to Bim Haskelovanovitch, though I could barely get his whole name on the postcard. "Lucky I wasn't bitten by anything yet. Grandpa says in Arizona everything sticks, stings, or stinks, but I love it and am getting a nice tan. Say 'o-hayo' to Hiroshi for me." O-hayo is the only word I know in Japanese, and it means either "Good morning" or "Good evening." Well, whatever; Hiroshi would understand.

When I wasn't writing postcards or playing croquet or swimming or eating, I worked on my James Watt report, and I finally did it: concentrated long enough to find out more than I ever wanted to know about the aurora borealis. Better late than never.

On the day before we left, Mom and Grandma and I went to the shopping mall, because Mom had promised me an Arizona t-shirt, Mom wanted to buy some souvenirs, and Grandma, believe it or not, had promised Edward a ceramic saguaro to stick in the bottom of his fish tank.

Off we went, and I found the shirt I wanted in about five minutes and kept hoping Mom and Grandma would be finished with their shopping in about another ten, but no luck. It's like they had to cover every inch of the mall before they could decide what to buy and for whom. I imagined my last day in the sun slipping away a mile a minute and then, suddenly, as I was dragging myself from window to window, trying not to yawn or keep asking what time it was, I saw the most beautiful sweater I'd ever seen in my life. It was on a mannequin in a store near the escalator on the second floor. It was dark blue, with little white specks knitted into it. I guess the reason I loved it was that it reminded me of the Arizona sky the way Dad and I had seen it two nights ago, although not one other person in the world might have noticed the similarity.

I just stood there staring at that sweater, my mouth practically watering, until Mom noticed me. "You like that sweater, don't you, Sunday? I do, too."

"I love it," I said.

She had been so nice to me since the Bianca Beaumont incident that I didn't want to take advantage of her by begging for it, but I'd never seen a sweater I'd liked better in my life.

Mom and Grandma went over to the mannequin to check the price of the sweater, which had a tag hanging from one sleeve, and of course it was very expensive. And of course Grandma offered to buy it for me for Christmas. And of course Mom refused to let her, saying that with Grandpa so near retirement, and five grandchildren to buy gifts for, it was out of the question. And then Mom said, "But you know, Sunday could use a beautiful sweater to go to auditions in," and she sort of stood there biting her lip and wavering.

My conscience started whapping me. Now, it said, tell her your auditioning days are through. Say it, go ahead. Be honest! But I couldn't say it. I couldn't say it and kiss that sweater good-bye forever. I made a quick, on-the-spot decision.

I'd go to another audition, or two, or more. Maybe give it until after Christmas. If I could hang in, Mom would be happy as anything, and I'd have a whole winter ahead wearing that sweater—wearing the Arizona sky on my back. Bite the bullet; the sweater was worth it.

As the salesclerk wrapped it up, I had a very short bout of hesitation, and then Mom said, "Remember, Sunday, this is to be considered your major Christmas present. Are you sure you really want it?"

"It's gorgeous," I said. "*Heavenly.*" I smiled. "Yes!"

"Well, you do look adorable in it, doesn't she, Grandma?"

Grandma gave me a big wink. "Awesome!" she laughed.

9

I LOVE going on trips, and I love coming home. Everything seems somehow different but the same, new yet familiar. I always feel, even if it's been just a few days, as if I've been gone a year.

I think everyone in my family feels exactly the same way; the minute we stepped through our front door, and even before we dragged the luggage upstairs, we all shot off in different directions.

Edward flew right to the fish tank and checked out Scamp, who looked as if he'd had a speedy recovery ("Feelin' better, Scamp? Wow! He's really moving! Great to see you back in shape!") and stuck the china saguaro in the middle of his bunched water plants at the bottom; Dad checked through the pile of mail that had accumulated on the floor of the hall while we were away ("It figures—one postcard, six bills, and six-hundred pieces of junk mail"); I got on the telephone and spoke to Karen ("Didn't see Stewart the whole time you were away but heard he got a virus and couldn't eat a bite of turkey. I didn't eat much of my Thanksgiving dinner, either, not that tempura is bad. Maybe if it had come with stuffing . . ."); and Mom checked the answering machine ("Please call the Farley Agency first thing Monday for an audition appointment Tuesday afternoon. It's for Lancelot Dog Food, and they're going to be needing a number of children").

Mom reported this message to me while I was sorting out my dirty summer clothes from my wrinkled but clean summer clothes. I tried to look as if she were relaying good news, but it wasn't easy. Mom thought I was thinking laundry, so the somber moment passed. We both agreed on one thing: rain, snow, sun, or wind, I would wear the new sweater. Mom said that it would Knock Them Dead, but I wasn't sure. I did hope it would Knock Stewart Dead, but I wasn't sure of that either. And for a minute, Mom hesitated about letting me wear it to school at all. I wore her down fast, by promising I would not drink or eat anything at lunch that could possibly put even a speck anywhere, including the sleeves. I also promised that if there were science experiments, I'd put on a smock or one of Dad's old shirts.

It turned out not to be necessary. The Whip was absent, probably home sick with the same bug Stewart had had—and maybe I'd had, too, and the substitute let us do whatever we wanted, which for me meant daydreaming about Stewart, although what I'd meant to do was go over my report on James Watt before handing it in. Stewart had flown right by me in the hall without noticing my sweater this morning, and so had the whole rest of the school, except Hiroshi, who said, "Nice swetta. Good on you," and told me Bim had showed him my postcard, and of course, Karen, who said it was beautiful and reminded her of Long Island Sound in winter (!). Everybody did notice my tan, though, and lots of kids remarked on my hair being lighter. Bim Haskelovanovitch said he'd once had a cat that turned that color before she died, but not to worry, I looked as if I'd last another year, at least. He also thanked me for my postcard.

Mom was waiting for me at the usual spot in front of school, looking a bit nervous; she'd left Edward with Mrs. Mlcik because Ziggy decided he couldn't make it at the last minute. Apparently, taking care of Edward's fish for a week had taken too much out of him; he'd called and said he was "too tired" to baby-sit. Mrs. Mlcik is a nice lady but speaks worse English than Hiroshi, and nobody is sure exactly what language it is she does speak. Mom says Serbo-Croatian, but Dad says Extra-Terrestrial.

I felt Edward could sit alone on a volcano for a week without anything happening to him as long as they put a TV up there, but Mom tends to be very cautious and left a list of numbers for Mrs. Mlcik to call, just in case. I am not sure Mrs. Mlcik speaks numbers, either, since she went to three wrong houses the first time she came to baby-sit for us (although our house number, 17, is right out there over the mail slot where nobody could miss it), but on the plus side, she can cook hamburgers that are so good they don't even need catsup.

On the way to the city and even once we were in the office loft in which these tryouts were being held, Mom was so distracted that she didn't do the usual brushing off of my shoulders, offering of breath mints, or telling me to comb my hair.

As soon as we walked in, I pushed through the crowds to the sign-up sheet like I'd done it a million times (I felt as if I really had), checked out the storyboard, and picked up a script. Obviously the girls who would be in this dog food commercial were not going to have many lines. They were supposed to be sitting in front of a fireplace, having sort of a winter picnic with the dog, who would leap up and run off, knocking everything on the rug all over the place with his tail. The girls—I think there were supposed to be about five of us—would let out little yelps and screams. One of us got to say, "Down, Boy!" but most of the dialogue went to a little boy chasing the dog.

Mom and I hadn't been there ten minutes when Heather and her mother walked in. It's hard to describe how I felt seeing her: happy to see a familiar, friendly face; sorry to have the competition. Maybe today, since there were to be so many girls chosen, we might both make it. Wishful thinking? Never mind. Today, she gave me a big smile as soon as she saw me, so I decided I was glad she was there.

As soon as she signed in, she and I went off to a little couch together while Mom and her mother settled in another corner. I told her how great she looked in the radial-tire commercial, and she said she hadn't seen it yet because she hardly got to watch TV at all. I wondered if I'd ever get to be that offhand about seeing myself on television. Not likely.

As usual, Heather was carrying her big, black, hard-cover book. "What is it that you're always reading?" I asked her. "It must really be interesting!"

"You bet it is!" she answered, and she showed it to me: a great big volume, filled with names of famous and important people, that told only one thing about each person —how he'd died. "Unbelievable!" I said, and turned the pages. I discovered that Mary, Queen of Scots, was beheaded with an ax, but the ax missed her neck the first time and just cracked her skull. Napoleon's Josephine got a gangrenous sore throat, whatever that is. Bessie Smith, an auto ace, bled to death. Queen Victoria's children said she'd dwindled to a "featherweight." "She had an all-white funeral," Heather whispered, rolling her eyes, and added, "You want to hear my favorite?" A lot of kids had gathered in the waiting room by this time, and she obviously didn't want to be overheard. "Virginia Woolf wanted to drown herself, so she just walked into the water, but it didn't work. She didn't sink. So you want to know what she did?"

I wasn't sure I wanted to know.

"She put rocks in the pockets of her coat and walked in again."

Ooh.

"And that did it. Wasn't that clever?"

"Isn't that a little gruesome?" I asked Heather.

She nodded very thoughtfully. "It's so fascinating, it keeps my mind busy, stops me from feeling nervous before an audition."

"I never thought you were capable of being nervous!"

"Of course I am. Like today. Look at this!" She pointed to a spot on her chin, right under her lip.

"What is it?"

"A zit. A great big zit! You mean you didn't notice it?"

"Not really."

"How could you miss it?"

"It's not that big, Heather."

"Mom's been putting Compound 74 QF on it. I hope the makeup will cover it. And look here—" She turned her face and pointed to a spot over her eyebrow. "I think I'm getting another one right here!"

"I don't think it's that noticeable, Heather, honestly."

"Let's hope it's not," Heather whispered.

❋   ❋   ❋

By this time, I could pick out quite a few familiar faces in the waiting room.

There was a red-haired boy, with more freckles than I have, whom I kept seeing at every audition, and a girl who wore glasses but whipped them off whenever the casting director appeared, and the same fifteen-year-old girl who looked like a twelve-year-old I'd seen at the Down Home Peanut Butter auditions. Little Todd appeared with what looked like a new haircut; had someone actually styled this five-year-old's hair with a ruler? It sure looked as if Mr. Paul himself had taken an hour to cut it straight, blow it dry, and part the perfect, measured part. I was beginning to feel as if we were a sort of loose-knit community. I also felt as if some of these kids were not too friendly and were eyeing each other, and me, as if we were carrying pipe bombs.

I'll admit the spirit of good will was not exactly flowering among us, but luckily Heather was not like that, and again, she and I were called in together, this time with four other girls and three little boys. My mom winked as we got up to go inside, and Heather's mother said, "You'll do fine, honey, you always do," as Heather passed, and she reached out to straighten the hem of her skirt.

I'm glad Mom knew enough not to make any public good-luck announcements or tugs, but I did see her do something she thought I missed: she crossed her fingers and stuck them under her pocketbook.

*   *   *

This casting studio was bigger, with wooden, planked floors and all sorts of wires snaking along them, lights hanging at different heights around the room, and tall windows that looked about three stories high. As we walked in, we announced our names and ages to the videotaping machine one at a time, answered a question or two—"Where do you go to school?"; "Was it a long ride from Scranton/Rye/Litchfield/Stanhope?"—and then we were told to "Let it all hang out!"

Someone had spread a blanket on the ground, smack in the middle of the floor, and that was where the girls were told to sit, in a semicircle, around what we were to pretend was a blazing fire in a ski lodge. It was supposed to be sort of an after-ski party.

This audition seemed to be run by a man who was wearing blue-tinted glasses that kept sliding down his nose. He kept smiling as if he loved this job, loved us, and loved blazing fires. Right away I liked him a lot better than Gray Beard. He also kept calling us "girlies." "Okay, girlies, you're drinking hot chocolate, grilling hot dogs, and offering a marshmallow to Rover. Rover isn't here today, but Miss Gargan will fill in. When Miss Gargan jumps up, you all scream and scatter. Right, girlies?"

Miss Gargan looked nothing like a dog, but she did her best in the middle of the blanket. She said, "arf-arf" and "bow-wow," and we laughed, and she laughed, and the man with the blue-tinted glasses smiled like crazy. She sat sort of scrunched over and then jumped up, and we did what we'd been told to do, scream and scatter. "Girlies! Girlies! That's not screaming! That's anemic gasping! Try and belt out a good one, okay?"

We did it, and we did it again.

Each time, he and Miss Gargan and another man stopped to confer. They looked us over one by one, they took notes, changed our positions, and then called the boys in, one at a time.

All three boys looked very shy and very young. One by one, they were told to run by our blanket chasing the dog, then stop, pant, and say the line, "My dog never runs out of energy when I feed him Lancelot Dog Chow."

One of the little boys was Todd, whose last name, I was to learn very soon, was O'Hanlon.

He ran past our blanket, stopped, panted, and said, "My dog never runs out of en-gery when I feed him Blandzalot . . . ."

Miss Gargan laughed. The man with the blue-lens glasses pushed them back up his nose and said, "Let's try that again, Toddy."

"My dog never runs out of engery."

"No, not *engery*, Toddy, *energy*. Say energy."

"Energy."

"Good. Now try the whole thing."

"My dog never runs out of energy when I feed him . . . when I feed him . . . ."

"Lancelot, Toddy."

Miss Gargan giggled.

"My dog never runs out of engery when I feel . . . I mean . . . ."

"Toddy! Concentrate, sweetheart. Take it slow. En-er-gy."

Toddy shook his well-cut head and tried it again. He kept looking down at his sneakers and tugging at his gray corduroy pants.

He tried again.

And again.

Miss Gargan and the man in the glasses kept smiling at each other, trying not to smile. He must have goofed eight times.

Finally, Miss Gargan said, "Come on, honey, shape up! You can *do* it!"

And the man in the glasses said, "Give it all you've got, Toddy!" and Todd's face went pink.

Then red. In fact, his face went so red it looked as if they'd made him up for a sunburn commercial.

We all saw it at the same time, the way his hands shot up to the front of his pants, and the way the light gray corduroy turned very dark, in one patch, right in front and along one leg.

And we all saw the look on his face.

Todd had wet his pants.

We tried not to laugh; at least, Heather and I did. Everybody else sort of gave in to it, and by the time Miss Gargan had led him off to the bathroom, his wet sneaker squishing along the floor, most of the girls were doubled over on the blanket, in hysterics.

"Poor kid," I said.

"You're not kidding. He'll never hear the end of this," Heather whispered.

And she was right. From that day on Todd stopped being called Todd. He became Puddles O'Hanlon. Maybe forever.

10

CHRISTMAS is always a big deal in our house, but that particular Christmas sort of came and went in a blur. I do remember that Karen and I teamed up to sell clay-bird tree ornaments made by the art department; I remember Christmas shopping like mad and helping Mom cut cookies shaped like stars and pine cones; I remember finally getting old enough to go to midnight church services; and I remember going to pick up Grandma Ericson at the airport.

She is my mother's mother and really different from my other grandma. She works for a cosmetics company and doesn't have time to cut cookies with a cookie cutter or bake anything, but she does have time to smell good and to look like a tall, white Christmas angel. Right at the airport she whispered she'd bought me a pair of earrings at her gentleman-friend's jewelry store right off

Lake Shore Drive in Chicago, which is where she lives, and when I put those shiny earrings shaped like wishbones in my ears, they'd bring me luck getting a part in a commercial.

She must have been right, because the best gift of all that Christmas was the one that came three days after New Year's—we got a callback!

The Farley Agency telephoned to tell Mom that I'd been chosen from a group of forty or fifty girls to re-audition for the Lancelot Dog Chow commercial, and to please be back at the same studio for further interviews on Wednesday at nine o'clock in the morning. Whoopee!

Now I was glad I'd stuck with it. A callback doesn't mean you've got the part, but it means someone was interested enough to give me another chance. Not everybody thought the way Gray Beard had!

Mom was even more excited than I was, but Dad played it cool. "Don't count your kibbles before they're hatched," he said. Edward was too busy naming his two new Dwarf Gouramis (Popeye and Olive) to make his usual nine-year-old's observations.

My collarbone weather report for the big day was that it was going to snow, so Mom decided we'd better not plan on driving. We'd get up very early and take the train instead. She set the alarm for six-thirty, but as it turned out, the alarm rang late. The snow had knocked out the power in the neighborhood and stopped the clocks. Luckily the power was out for only half an hour so we made the train, but there was no time to blow-dry my hair. This turned out to be the cloud with a silver lining, but it seemed like a disaster at the time.

Dad kissed me as Mom and I were leaving and wished me luck. He also said I should not be going out with a wet head. Edward, after asking Mom if she'd put flavored marshmallows in his lunch bag and what flavors, asked how come *I* was allowed to go out with a wet head while *he* had to wear a yukky rain hat, also wished me luck. As I put on my Arizona sweater and my gold wishbone earrings—and *my* yukky wool hat—I took a minute to do what I'd seen Mom do in the Lancelot audition waiting room two weeks ago—cross my fingers—and wish *myself* luck.

If only I'd brought more than my French verbs textbook to wait with. As the kids poured into the waiting room, I could concentrate on only one thing: trying to keep myself relaxed and my knees steady. There were fewer kids than last time but still enough, and Mom was worried about my still-damp hair, which didn't help. Pneumonia was on her mind, not to mention how I looked. She'd pulled a comb through it in the ladies' room, but although the snow outside had stopped, the weather was cold, and unless I sat near the radiator for four hours, I'd still look like a wet mop at the audition.

And then Heather walked in and my first thought was,

hey, great! And I waved her over right away so we could talk and make the time pass together and get my hair off my mind. Heather kindly said she liked the way it looked damp, but she wasn't fooling anybody.

Of course, she had her big book with her, and practically the first thing she told me was that she discovered that poor Walt Disney had died of cancer at sixty-five, which was exactly the same age her own grandfather had died of cancer, and that Ernest Hemingway had shot himself right here—she pointed to a spot directly above her left eyebrow—and that's when I had my second thought. Just where she was pointing, and you couldn't miss it, was a big, red splotch. I guess the Compound 74 QF wasn't working; Heather's skin was breaking out. Although the zit on her chin had disappeared, another two had appeared under her lip.

Of course, I didn't say a word about it.

"Did you ever hear of Jimmy Dean?" Heather was asking me.

"No."

"He was an actor. He died very young. An automobile crash broke his neck."

"Terrible."

"And you know what the name of the person was whose car hit Jimmy's?"

"No."

"Turnupspeed."

89

"You're kidding."

"No, really."

"Wow."

"Is Heather boring you with that morbid book?" Heather's mother suddenly joined us and began lightly brushing invisible lint from the shoulders of Heather's striped sweater. I immediately assured her that it was helping to get my mind off my un-dried hair, when she came up with what turned out to be an incredible/great/ phenomenal idea. A dynamite/showbiz idea!

"Why don't you braid your hair?" she suggested. "Into one big, long braid!"

Mom wasn't sure. I wasn't sure. Even Heather looked thoughtful, until we tried it. We borrowed a rubber band from the office receptionist and went into the ladies' room to give the idea a shot.

Then, it was unanimous. We all thought the braid, which was so long it went past the middle of my sweater in back, was a great improvement over the wet straggles. Not only that, it was different. None of the other girls wore their hair that way. It made me a little more distinctive. And the first thing Miss Gargan said when we trooped back into the studio was, "Hey, I like your braid, Sunday. It's crisp and neat. A great idea."

I did pretty well at this audition. I had more confidence.

I screamed louder. I really put my heart and soul into the scene. I noticed that little Todd had not been asked back. A new kid, Chip Heldorf, was saying Todd's line and pronouncing "energy" and "Lancelot" without any trouble.

When Heather and I walked out of the audition together, I felt as if I was still moving in a bright light. Just the way Miss Gargan smiled when she handed Mom back my composite, and the little tug she gave my braid, gave me a really warm feeling.

Until I caught Heather's mother's face. Heather's expression was cool as usual, but her mother's was grim. Being a professional, she could probably tell that this was one commercial Heather wouldn't be asked to appear in, just by the way Miss Gargan returned her photographs and said, "Thank you for coming." Maybe it was my imagination, but it seemed to me that when Heather's mother looked at Heather, she looked right at her chin, her forehead over her eyebrow, and under her lip.

I said good-bye and asked Heather to write her telephone number on a slip of paper. She took mine, too, and we promised to call if either of us got another callback or any other news. As we left the building, we all said good-bye, and Mom said, "Have a happy New Year," and Heather's mother sort of shook her head and sighed and instead of saying, "Happy New Year to you, too," she said, "I hope so, but I doubt it. I really doubt it."

Although I hardly paid attention to the comment then, I remembered the remark later, and in fact, all through spring and into summer, I couldn't get it out of my mind.

The Whip was up to his old tricks. "We have a new year and I have a new philosophy. I will describe it in three words: 'You Will Work.'"

It sounded a lot like his last year's philosophy, and in fact, everybody groaned like they'd heard it before. Out came the assignments in batches and bunches. He was overflowing with post-holiday pep.

The callback had meant missing a crucial lesson in The Heavens, which was to be the topic with which he intended to bug us until still another new topic occurred to him. My first assignment was to make up for the class I'd missed by copying all the notes he'd given on celestial navigation and to read up on ancient sky myths in the textbook.

I had intended to invite Stewart over to untrim the tree, which had already dropped enough needles to make a wreath on the rug, but now that was out of the question. I'd also been asked by Madame Popindreau to learn a French poem of my choice, and my language-arts teacher suddenly got it into her head we'd be reading a new book every two weeks. When Karen asked if I wanted to team up selling oranges and grapefruits from Florida door-to-door, I had to turn her down.

Karen said she'd ask Erin Wurtzel, who wasn't that new anymore, and was in great demand socially since her parents bought her the most glamorous videotaping machine for Christmas anybody had ever seen.

I told Karen I'd probably be able to sell jams and jellies with her in February or March, when things eased up, but I had the feeling they weren't going to ease up that fast. Mom had found a sort of talent academy not far from where we live, where she hoped I'd start classes in acting and speech in February, if we could fit it into my schedule. "We have to think professional," she said.

It occurred to me that "thinking professional" was a new phrase Mom probably picked up from Heather's mother. Since I was really getting into the swing of things, had had a callback, and might really finally get an honest-to-goodness part, in a way it was like the tug I get in my collarbone before we're going to have a heavy rain. Although I liked the sound of "professional," something tugged. Something made me uneasy.

11

IT'S a funny thing, but all the blue sweaters and wishbone earrings couldn't seem to do what that braid did for me.

"You got it, you got the part!" Mom was waiting at the door for me less than a week later when I came home from school, and her face was shining as if someone had a pink spotlight on it. "They thought you were adorable! They kept mentioning the braid!"

I said I didn't believe it about twenty-five times and Mom said it was true and that she'd put in a call to Dad in Hartford and left a message that said: "Sunday made it! Didn't I always tell you she would?"

Edward was home with a sore throat that day, not in bed, exactly, but on the couch, watching television, and he said he'd predicted I'd be a TV star and wasn't it lucky he'd stayed home and not missed the excitement? But now he was dying and could Mom stop making calls long enough to bring him some chocolate chip ice cream to soothe his throat?

"Hello, Heather!" I'd expected that her voice might sound far away or weak, but no. Heather sounded as if she were talking on the upstairs extension. Mom said I could make the long-distance call if we didn't make it into a marathon.

"I got it, I got the part!" I screamed. If I got to live eighty more years and they asked me to look back on my life and tell which was the happiest moment so far, this was definitely it. "Did they call you, too?" No, they hadn't called, she said, and then I think there was the slightest sliver of silence before she congratulated me. She said she was truly happy for me and knew I'd do a good job, and she said she'd watch for the commercial and give me an honest opinion of my performance. She said she'd buy Lancelot Dog Chow even if she never got a dog. She sounded enthusiastic through and through, but there was something flat in her voice, as if she were trying for a key that was too high and not quite making it. Not quite making it was something new to Heather, although this was not her first rejection; she'd told me of the many times she'd tried out for parts that went to someone who just happened to be shorter or younger, or who looked more like the people the casting company had already chosen to play her parents or brothers or sisters.

This was a different rejection. One day in some waiting room or other I'd heard two girls discussing seeing a recent photograph of the kid who'd played Cousin Mindy for about three years. She'd hit Transition. To TV kid performers, that's a word about as pleasant as Sludgepit. Falling into the Transition stage is what happened to Cousin Mindy, whose looks changed as she began getting older. She didn't get zits—she just stopped looking cute and kid-like, and started getting a little strange and thin-looking, as if they'd taken the original and put her on a rack and stretched her out. Nobody would buy Little Farms Oatmeal slurped by a kid in Transition. Some kids got fat or awkward, some had voices that began to go up and down like power tools, but this is what they all had in common: Transition kids were about as much in demand as wet tennis balls.

Was Heather worried? I couldn't tell for sure, but I remembered her mother's words about the new year.

"I'll probably see you at another tryout before I even get to film this commercial," I said, keeping it cheery. Nothing was going to get me down tonight—not even the thought of Heather's disappointment.

"Oh, absolutely," Heather said brightly, and then she said she'd better hang up because this conversation was costing a fortune. Since it was *our* fortune, the message was clear. Heather wanted to get off the telephone and not talk about it. Who could blame her?

Karen, on the other hand, was really excited. She had to hear every detail. When/where/how/who? She couldn't wait to see me on the tube and would tell all her relatives, coast-to-coast, that the girl in the Lancelot Dog Chow commercial was her very best friend!

"I have one little favor to ask you," I said, lowering my voice so Mom and Edward couldn't hear.

"What is it?"

"If you see Stewart tomorrow, just sort of make sure he finds out, will you?"

Concentrating in school became no easy job. French verbs are not that fascinating to begin with, and as far as I was concerned the best thing about The Heavens were the stars, on which I could make wishes: I wanted the time to fly so that next Monday, the day of the filming, would be here fast, and just as important, I wanted to dazzle Stewart. His jaw had dropped a whole inch, Karen reported, when she told him during lunch. He told her that his own dog, Home Run, ate Lancelot Dog Chow regularly and particularly liked their liver-flavored, iron-enriched chow. He said he'd watch for me.

On the day of the filming, Dad called from Burlington to wish me "break a leg" and tell me he'd spent all last night bragging about me to his business associates at dinner. Mom said she just couldn't believe how casually I was taking everything and how calm I was, considering this was my honest-to-goodness "opening night"—though it was seven in the morning.

Of course, I wasn't really calm. My blood pressure felt like it was up there in the four digits, and for the first time since I was about seven years old, I actually felt carsick driving into the city.

I still felt a little queasy when we arrived at the film location, which turned out to be the surprise of surprises. Imagine walking into a city apartment on the fourteenth floor of an old building, into someone's living room that was furnished to look like a ski house in Vermont, complete with fireplace, logs, Indian rug, a deerhead with antlers, and a big screen in the corner that hid the part of the room that didn't look like a ski lodge. A sort of fake log wall had been set up, too, and skis and poles were leaning against that, and in the other corner—I had to blink a couple of times to make sure I wasn't imagining this—was an incredible buffet spread, a sort of a combination of breakfast and lunch, as if this were going to be a big party instead of a day of hard work.

The director of the commercial, Mr. Rutledge, was munching on a bagel and drinking coffee, and he waved us over to the refreshments immediately. "Had your breakfast?" he asked Mom and me. Two of the other kids had arrived and were already digging in. "Don't get sugar on your ski clothes," the wardrobe lady warned. They were already dressed to look as if they'd just come off the slopes.

The mound of doughnuts looked as if it was intended to feed six families for two weeks, and I wasn't even tempted until I saw a chocolate one I knew Edward would love. I took it and, when no one was looking, wrapped it in a napkin and stuck in into the canvas bag that held my extra clothes.

We'd been instructed to bring a heavy sweater, ski pants, and ski boots, and although the wardrobe lady said my dark blue sweater was perfect, I had no boots or ski pants, so she sent me into a little bedroom that had been turned into a dressing room, to try on some ski pants she'd brought along, and she handed me a tall pair of furry *après*-ski boots that looked two sizes too big. A friendly Chinese girl, who was going to be sitting next to me in the commercial, and I spent about twenty minutes trying on this and that until the wardrobe lady voted on light blue ski pants for me and leg warmers for the Chinese girl. A hairdresser appeared with a comb in one hand and a blow dryer in another and said the boots looked dynamite, but not to trip over the electric cords that were lying all over the floor. She rebraided my hair and said that was dynamite, too. I made a mental note that if I was going to be in show business, I'd have to stop saying "awesome" and start saying "dynamite."

* * *

99

All this time Mom had been sitting in a folding chair near the buffet and filling out forms. Later she told me she'd never written on so many dotted lines in her life—tax forms, releases, contracts—and that with all the commotion, it was really hard even to remember our phone number, let alone my brand-new social security number.

There really was commotion!

I'd thought filming a commercial would be one-two-three fast, the way it appears on our television screen—a few rehearsals, then a director screaming "Take One!," and five or ten minutes of being filmed, but I had a lot to learn; what takes about thirty seconds on the screen took us pretty nearly eight hours before we got it right, and there was some talk about coming back the next day if the dog didn't settle down!

That St. Bernard was the best part of filming that commercial. His name was Mango, and he was the biggest dog I think I've ever seen in my life, but instead of looking ferocious, he looked as if he were smiling. In fact, I thought he might have been sampling some of the brandy in the flask his owner had tied around his neck before we started filming. He kept wagging his tail and barking and edging over to the buffet. We all wanted to brush him and pet him and play with him, all except Chip Heldorf, who took one look at Mango and went flying into his mother's arms. She tried to calm Chip down and almost succeeded, but when the camera started rolling and we all thought he'd calmed down, he couldn't say, "My dog never runs out of energy, etc," unless Mango's owner was holding him by the collar with both hands. The minute the dog bounded toward the dog food in the dish near Chip's feet the way he was supposed to, Chip's eyes started to roll and his chin started to tremble.

Mr. Rutledge was losing patience. He was wearing striped suspenders and kept pulling one and then the other. "The dog won't hurt you, Chip! He's not a *lion!*" I think he said it about a hundred times. "Now let's calm down and try again, okay?"

Chip nodded. Mango was actually very well-behaved. He watched his owner's hand signals from behind the camera and thumped his tail on the floor and looked so cute we all wanted to take him home with us—except, as I said, Chip.

He began again, "My dog never runs out of energy . . . ," and then he stopped. Mango, on a hand signal, came bounding along, looking as if he were having the time of his life, ready to dive into his dish of Lancelot Dog Chow. He looked as if his whole body were wagging, not only his tail, probably for the same reason this segment had to be filmed first—because he was very, very hungry.

Chip panicked. He stumbled backward, tipped over the chair behind him, and when it crashed to the floor, he burst into tears.

Mr. Rutledge pulled at his suspenders and let them snap against his chest. Ow. I could practically feel it.

He shook his head. "Oh, for God's sake! Okay—I give

up! Where's the backup?" he cried. Then he used a very bad word.

A backup is a kid hired to be on hand just in case someone gets sick or doesn't show up. I didn't even realize that the little kid I'd seen with a mother sitting near mine was a possible replacement for Chip—sort of an understudy.

Chip was really in hysterics now. His mother couldn't calm him down; he had thrown himself against her arm and buried his face in her sleeve.

"It's only a dog, darling; he won't hurt you," she kept saying, but finally she gave up. A few minutes later, still dressed in ski clothes, still sobbing, Chip left with his mother, and the backup did the scene. Of course we had to wait while he rehearsed it, and while they found him a pair of ski pants and sweater, and while the hairdresser brushed his hair.

As far as our few seconds on camera went, we must have filmed our sequence twenty-five times. A lady with a stopwatch around her neck kept telling us we were running over, and the lighting man kept seeing shadows on our faces and readjusting lights, and once the telephone rang in the other room, and then the fire in the fireplace died down, and when they added more logs the room got too smoky.

At one o'clock another mouth-watering feast was set up for lunch. A caterer actually brought in steak and baked potatoes and strawberry shortcake. The kids got orange soda and ice cream, too.

When we went at it again after lunch, one of the skis fell down with a crash and interrupted one take, and then Mr. Rutledge decided we were sitting too close to one another and rearranged our positions, and then someone sneezed during another take. By the time we got it right, I was pretty hoarse from letting out those screams, and I couldn't stop yawning. Obviously there was a lot more to making commercials than just saying a line and collecting a big check, and by the time we were finished, I felt the way I guess Dad feels when he crashes in for the weekend after a week on the road.

I was half asleep by the time we got home, but I still thought of my day as one big, long party.

"How was it?" Edward asked me as soon as we walked through the front door. "Was it fun?"

I handed him his doughnut and really got a kick out of the way his eyes lit up when he took the first bite. "It was dynamite," I said.

12

IT'S hard to believe, but before that commercial ever appeared on television, I went to three more auditions and six more callbacks—five for the same part, which I finally got! It was a toothpaste commercial filmed in someone's bathroom, and I was supposed to be teaching a kid brother how to brush with Wintermint Toothpaste. I got to say, "Pay attention, Tyler! A little Wintermint goes a long way. Oh, Tyler, not that way. Brush up and down! And don't lose the cap, Tyler!"

Puddles O'Hanlon got the part of Tyler, and this time he had no trouble with his only line, "Say, this stuff tastes like peppermint!" But Puddles had other problems. He had just turned six and had lost his first tooth, so they had to replace it with a removable fake. Even up close you couldn't tell the difference, although Puddles said he couldn't eat with it, and was also scared of swallowing it. I felt really sorry for him.

Every time I had an interesting experience during an audition or filming, I couldn't wait to get to school to tell Karen and the rest of the kids about it. At first, everyone seemed very interested, but little by little, I began to notice that although they listened politely, the kids couldn't really understand what my other life was like. The February school money-raising project was a flea market in the gym and it seemed all everybody ever talked about.

Every afternoon after school the kids went door-to-door collecting junk people had no more use for, and every day at lunch they described the "very slightly chipped" water pitchers or the 1932 ironing board someone had donated and the incredible fortunes some rich collector was going to pay for them. Since I hardly had time to do homework these days, and was even missing school now and then, I couldn't join in. I really felt out of it.

Until my big day came.

It was seven-thirty on a Tuesday night and the telephone rang. "I saw you, I saw you!" It was Karen, and she was reporting the airing of the Lancelot commercial, which had appeared on channel seven right after the station break. "You were only on for a second, but you looked gorgeous!" She went on and on about how awesome it was to see her best friend right on the screen and how professional I looked and how the sweater looked lighter blue in person than on the screen and what a cute dog Mango was. I'd been upstairs trying to catch up on French verbs and had missed it!

Of course, I ran into the den to tell Mom and Edward, who had been watching some science show on the educational channel and hadn't seen it, either, but before I could get the words out, the telephone rang again. This time it was Heather.

All these weeks I'd been hoping I'd run into her at auditions the way I used to, but she'd disappeared, and I was a little afraid to call her at home. I was worried she'd think I'd called to brag about all my assignments while she wasn't getting any.

"You were only on for a few seconds, but you played the part perfectly," Heather said, in her usual all-together way.

"I was really all right?"

"Very professional."

"Oh, thank goodness!"

"I'll bet you're going to go places! I'll bet your career is really going to take off!"

I decided that asking how *her* career was coming was less rude than not asking.

I expected a gloomy answer, but she surprised me completely. "You haven't seen me these last few weeks because my skin was breaking out like crazy," she said.

106

"That's what I thought, and I'm really sorry, Heather," I quickly put in.

"But now it's going to be all right! My mother took me to a big skin specialist in New York, and I've started this new serum vitamin A treatment. He also gave me a brand-new miracle ointment, and he promised my skin would be clear in two weeks."

"How wonderful!"

"So we'll be seeing each other just like always!" Heather promised.

It really was great news. I'd missed having a friend who understood the business, someone I could really confide in. "I'm so glad you called!" I said, and she said it was a sure thing we'd see each other very soon.

Although not all the kids at school had seen the commercial, enough had to get everyone buzzing. The minute I walked into school, the "bow-wows" started, Bim asked me about snow conditions on the slopes, and during lunch in the cafeteria the kids pulled off a big joke on me.

I sat down at my usual table, and suddenly it seemed there were extra kids pulling up chairs and gathering around. I felt like a real celebrity, with everyone watching every move I made and listening to every word I had to say. I admit I absolutely loved the attention.

A paper cover from a straw came flying at me from the direction of the jocks' table near the window. "How ya doin'?" It was Stewart, who had sent it sailing to get my attention and now came over to tell me he'd come in too late from basketball practice to "catch my act" last night but heard I was great. He sat down right next to me and asked me if I could get a job for Home Run in the next Lancelot commercial.

I was a little flustered and started to tell him about Chip Heldorf, but he interrupted. "Aren't you going to eat today?" He was pulling a sandwich out of his brown paper bag, so it didn't seem like a strange question, but when I reached into my lunchbag to pull out the sandwich Mom had made for me, I felt something peculiar inside.

When I got it out and took a look, I felt my face go the color of dog chow: someone had replaced my ham and Swiss on rye with a little cellophane sack of Lancelot super-enriched dogmeal. It probably happened during Home Room, or maybe when I left my desk for a few minutes during language arts. And instead of my usual apple or cookie, I found two dog crackers shaped liked bones.

Now everybody practically fell off chairs laughing, and I let out a few hahas, too, but I laughed less. They weren't being mean, but I suppose I was embarrassed to be the butt of a joke, even if it was a good-natured one. And I don't know why, but it bothered me that Karen was in on it, too, and hadn't tipped me off that practically half the cafeteria would be doubled over at my expense.

Of course, I recovered almost immediately. I told

myself to stop being so sensitive and said, "Stewart, give this to Home Run with my compliments," and I handed him one of the dog biscuits. "And I'll eat the other one," I said, and the kids cheered. I'd laughed with them and carried it off; after all, these were my friends, and they liked me.

At least, they liked me for the moment.

The next day my first check came; it was Saturday and Dad was at home. We were eating brunch, and he brought it in with the rest of the mail, and after he opened the envelope and showed it to Mom, he conducted a little ceremony.

He poured orange juice into all our glasses so we could toast my success. Edward raised his glass and said he couldn't believe how much money I'd gotten for three seconds' work. He said it was enough for a new fish tank, a new heater, and a year's supply of live food, and he'd have to deliver papers for the rest of his life to make money like that. What was I going to do with all that cash?

I said it was enough for a hundred Bermuda bags but all I wanted was one, with my initials embroidered on it. I'd wanted one for a long time, preferably in navy blue and red. I might even have my whole first name embroidered across the front.

I'd always wanted to be called Jenny or Lynne or Karen, to have some nice, ordinary name, but now I felt as if maybe I was living up to my mother's distinguished choice—at last. I visualized "Sunday" in scrolled script— very distinctive. I'd carry it everywhere.

Dad had other ideas. I knew what they'd be even before he made the announcement. "College," he said, and he set down his empty glass in a way that meant business. He said we would not touch a bit of this money and would not allow me to "fritter" it away now. It was to go into a trust for my education, not for Bermuda bags.

There was no arguing with Dad once his mind was made up, so later I pleaded with Mom. She was in such a great mood these days that she was a pushover and said she'd work on it for me. Dad is much more likely to listen to her.

Sure enough, on Monday morning, she slipped a few bills into my hand. "Dad said, 'Okay, just this first time, as sort of a celebration.' I think you deserve it," she added, and she said she'd drive me to the shopping center on Wednesday after school so we could pick one out.

For the rest of my life, I'll never understand what got into me that Wednesday afternoon. After telling everybody in school about my soon-to-be-bought Bermuda bag, discussing colors, monogram styles with Karen and Erin, after looking forward Monday, Tuesday, and Wednesday to going to the store and actually ordering it, I suddenly decided that a Bermuda bag wasn't what I wanted at all.

What I wanted all of a sudden was a weird-looking, orange, flat-nosed fish with bulgy eyes, the most expensive tropical fish in the shopping center pet store: a lion-fish. It was in the window of Pet City, and we just happened to pass it on our way to the department store. I wanted to buy it for Edward, who had once told me he'd seen one in a magazine, that he thought it was the most beautiful fish in the world, and that when he grew up and got very rich, he would buy one just like it. He kept the magazine under his bed and looked at the picture of the fish again and again.

My mother couldn't get over it. "I knew it, the moment you were born. You *are* special," she said when I'd left all my Bermuda bag money in the pet store, and she'd even had to chip in four dollars and sixty cents to cover the difference. "No other child would have done what you just did." Her eyes actually welled up.

I think she gave me too much credit. I knew Edward sometimes felt out of things, maybe was even a little lonely. I think being overweight made him shy around kids. A lot of times he was like a spectator on the side-lines, watching his friends play in Little League and never playing, watching the excitement of my new life without being a real part of it, and watching the life-and-death struggles of the fish in his tank. There would be other checks coming for me and other opportunities to buy Bermuda bags, but I might never see a lion-fish in this pet store again.

"It's no big deal," I said, and I can't explain it, but I

felt absolutely wonderful. I didn't have my monogrammed bag, but I had everything else. It was February, it was cold, it was slushy and grim. But holding the carefully wrapped jar with the lion-fish swimming inside and heading home in Mom's old red Toyota, I felt I had it all.

13

├──┤

IT was less than two weeks later that I woke up in the
middle of the night and lay there for about five minutes wondering what had awakened me. Nothing hurt,
there had been no explosion or thunder, and even my
collarbone wasn't twinging. Why was I up at this hour
when I'd crashed in with exhaustion not two hours before?

It had been a terrible day. The Whip had called me to
his desk after class and tore my latest test paper into four
equal pieces in front of my eyes. His silver pen flashed
the message that I was only giving a quarter of the effort
I should be giving in science, that he would not accept
this latest test flunk—58, and that if things didn't im-
prove immediately I was in danger of failing the course.

I'd rushed home and studied for a retest, trying to
memorize the names of all the required constellations of

the Southern Sky, but I also had to translate four impossibly hard paragraphs for French and prepare a book report outline for language arts. Language arts has always been one of my favorite subjects, but I was even falling down in that. It's hard to write a book report when you haven't had time to read the book.

Lying in the dark now, constellations, French verbs, and book themes floated through my head—as well as the lines of the Coco Balm sunburn commercial I'd auditioned for the day before.

Then I heard voices. Mom's bedroom door was open, and she was on the phone with Grandma. Ah, that was it; Grandma always called from Illinois late at night, after the rates changed. Of course, I couldn't hear Grandma's side of the conversation, but I did hear Mom's, although it wasn't my intention to listen but only to get back to sleep as fast as I could. It was getting harder and harder to get up in the morning these days.

Obviously, Grandma had called to tell Mom she'd seen the toothpaste commercial, and I could tell by the tone of Mom's remarks that Grandma was really impressed by it. ("Yes, she is a remarkable child." "Well, I was the one who always said she had a great deal of talent.") There was nothing new about phone calls from relatives; my Arizona grandparents had called Sunday to tell me they'd already seen the commercial three times and were becoming known by their neighbors as people who couldn't stop talking about their star granddaughter. Uncle Walter had called, too, to tell Dad he was going to buy stock in Wintermint Toothpaste and that his kids were running around the neighborhood bragging about their cousin on TV, and we suddenly got a letter from a great-aunt of Mom's in Wisconsin, who'd gotten a phone call from a distant cousin in Atlanta with the big news that I was a performer headed right for the top!

If I'd expected acclaim, this was it: Stewart had biked home with me twice last week, Bim asked me if I'd team up for the March attic-cleaning fund raiser, Erin Wurtzel had offered to let me use her new video recorder, and last Monday morning, while I was sitting cross-legged on the gym floor doing aerobic warmups with my class, the principal of the school, Mrs. Bealey (a.k.a. Mrs. Beastly), came over to tell me that she'd heard I was wonderful in a toothpaste commercial and to wish me luck in my future acting career. Then, she actually smiled. It is a known fact that the only time Mrs. Beastly has been seen to smile was in 1973, when the governor of the state visited the school.

I finally heard my mother hang up, telling my grandmother that she had already looked into it, and I still couldn't fall asleep. What had my mother looked into?

Now I heard Dad's voice, which sounded about as sleepy as I felt. "What have you looked into?" he asked Mom, as if he were able to read my mind right through the wall.

Acting school. Not Talent Academy, but another school

115

like it. The best, Mom was saying. Didn't we just get that very nice, fat check?

"College," Dad reminded Mom. "We agreed." He no longer sounded sleepy.

Mom reminded Dad that if I weren't making money now, he'd still have to send me to college. And wasn't acting school a good investment for the future, too?

Dad's voice got a bit louder. He felt that spending my money on acting or dancing lessons would be a mistake. After high school, it might be a different story, if acting were going to be my final career choice.

Mom said that if I wanted to keep up with other kids in my field, I needed every advantage.

Dad said he couldn't take it that seriously because he didn't think doing TV commercials was going to be my future.

Mom wanted to know how he could predict that; did he have a crystal ball?

I cringed under my covers. I do not like my parents to fight. It makes me feel just the way I felt when we were driving into the city the morning of the Wintermint filming—carsick.

Dad said, "This whole career thing of Sunday's is getting a little out of hand."

Mom said, "You're hardly at home, and when you are here I don't think you're aware enough of how important this really is to your daughter!"

Dad said, "To you, you mean!"

Mom said, "To everybody!"

Then Dad said that being away from home was not his choice. He had to make a living, didn't he?

And Mom's voice went up, as if she were addressing a crowd, and she said she wished he'd find a job where he wouldn't have to be gone so much.

There was a pause, and then Dad, because he hates fights, too, and really loves Mom, apologized. "Let's discuss it tomorrow, okay?" he said.

And Mom, because she loves Dad, said she was sorry she'd gotten so emotional, but she did wish he were around more.

Later, their door closed and the house got very quiet.

Finally, I fell asleep.

Edward named his lion-fish Rex. Rex is another name for King, and I had the feeling that Edward had secretly named the fish after himself—the highest honor!

To say he was overjoyed with his present is the understatement of understatements. Not only did he shoot over to his tank every day after school (without having his chocolate banana or cookies or ice cream first), but he invited the kids in the neighborhood to come by and see "the best swimmer in Connecticut."

On the day we got the knockout news from Mr. Farley, he was running around the fish tank taking pictures with Dad's Japanese camera and trying not to get the flashbulb to glare on the glass.

He hardly heard the news: this was no ordinary call-back. I was seriously being considered as one of two girls to appear in the Coco Balm sunburn lotion commercial. That in itself was fantastic, but the surprise icing on this cake was that this commercial was going to be filmed on location in Florida, and the actors and the whole crew were going to be flying down to Boca Raton—all expenses paid!

I would have another tryout, hopefully a final one, and had to report to the Monaco Casting Office on Fifth Avenue and Thirty-eighth Street at nine sharp next Tuesday morning.

If I had trouble concentrating on French verbs or constellations before, now it was as if my body were still moving through the halls of Stanhope High School but my head was already down on some white, sandy beach in Florida.

Mom kept telling me to please not neglect my schoolwork, and she offered to hear my verbs and help in any way she could, but I think even she was sort of dazed with what was happening. In fact, one day she came into the kitchen carrying two bags of groceries, and as Edward and I began to help her unwrap the stuff she'd bought, she started laughing.

"Look at this!" She pulled out two sacks of radishes and put them on the counter. "What's funny about two sacks of radishes?" I asked.

Mom walked over to the refrigerator and opened the

vegetable crisper drawer. Inside was still another sack of radishes, unopened.

"Why do you keep buying those?" I asked.

Mom was really laughing hard now. "I can't concentrate on what I'm doing in the supermarket because someone always stops me to say they've seen you on TV!"

"And that's why you buy *radishes*?"

"Well, today I met Mrs. Doeppel, and she's always been a snob! She hardly ever even said hello to me before, and now, just when I was picking up salad greens, she practically came running down the aisle to congratulate me on having such a remarkable daughter. 'Remarkable'— her adjective. For a minute I thought she was going to give me a kiss right there, at the produce scale! I was so thunderstruck I'm lucky I didn't grab two more sacks!"

"Next time I hope she catches you at the bakery counter, Mom!" Guess-Who put in.

"That's where the minister's wife caught me last week! And *she* said she hadn't realized there was a celeb in the parish!"

When Mom giggles, she seems to really put herself into it. She shakes and wobbles, and her face gets pink. "*Her* noun—*celeb!*"

"Well, Mom, how does it feel to be the mother of a celeb?"

Mom put down the radishes, and she came over to me and gave me a big bear hug. "It feels good, darling. In fact, I think it's fantastic!" she said.

14

ALTHOUGH I did predict precipitation for the day of the audition, I didn't know that it would be a nasty sleet that hit the streets like glass splinters. I didn't guess that I'd wake up with a nasty sore throat, that Ziggy, Edward's baby-sitter, would call early in the morning to cancel because he woke up with a sore throat, too, and that Mom would spend twenty frantic minutes trying to get hold of Mrs. Mlcik, who refused to take her car out of the driveway in this weather but finally agreed to come over in a taxi, if one was available on a day like this.

It was touch-and-go, but Mom managed everything and had us on the train at seven forty-two, right on the button. I tried to relax, but Mom kept looking at her watch, worrying whether the trains were running late and whether we'd be able to find a taxi in New York in sleet and rain.

I had other worries I didn't want to blab out (she was nervous enough): I was missing a big social-studies test, my science retest was due day after tomorrow (I still hadn't studied enough), and my book report on *Of Mice and Men* was already a week late.

There was more: the kids had spent practically the whole weekend putting prices on the junk they'd collected door-to-door, had painted and repaired some of it, cleaned and polished and dusted other stuff, and generally worked very hard to make the big sale a success. I didn't have a minute to spare, what with all the schoolwork I'd fallen behind in, not to speak of the special appointment Mom had arranged for me with Mr. Paul so he could cut off a few split ends and arrange some wispies around the hairline. He kept telling me that he'd known the minute Mom showed him my picture that I'd make it big, and he hoped that when I went up for my Oscar in a few years, he'd be allowed to do my hair for the Academy Awards ceremonies.

After my not showing up to work at school over the weekend, the kids seemed cool on Monday, or maybe I just imagined it. It turned out that Hiroshi had been given an Italian print in a broken frame, and while everybody kept trying to figure out the name of the artist in case he was an Old Master and this etching would turn out to be worth millions, the head of the art department came in and took one look and nearly fainted—the picture was a worthless print, but he said the frame was antique vermeil and worth even more than the old mink stole Bim's aunt had donated in order to get a tax deduction.

Obviously, with that much excitement, my audition did not seem like high drama. The kids were pretty bored with my stories, and they seemed all of a sudden to be closing me out.

Karen said I was imagining it, but even she was suddenly a little out of reach. At lunch, she and Erin were in a huddle half the time, and when I asked her to come over to my house Monday afternoon so we could do homework together, she couldn't make it because she and Erin were going to the local paper to see if they could get free publicity for the big sale.

Luckily, Stewart still seemed interested.

"How ya doin', Sunday?" he called after me when I was leaving school Monday. It was too cold to bike, so we walked to the bus together. He threw a couple of pebbles at the high branch of a tree and made a couple of perfect hits. He'd gotten a lot taller recently, and it wasn't only my imagination; Karen and Erin both said he was definitely the best-looking boy in school. "I got something to show you," he said with a mysterious smile, and he patted his rear jeans pocket as if he'd stashed some other valuable antique back there (another picture frame?) out of the reach of thieving pickpockets and the rest of the nosy world.

He sat next to me on the bus and asked how my career

was going, and would I be doing any more of those great dog-food spots?

I told him about tomorrow's Coco Balm audition, the possible trip to Florida, and recited the line I would have to say: "Ow, Mommy, this sunburn hurts so much!" and later, "I feel so much better now, I guess I'll go back to the beach and play some volleyball!"

Stewart seemed impressed, and finally he leaned forward and pulled a yellow envelope out of the back pocket.

"I knew you'd want to see these. They just came back from the developer. Aren't they great?"

He'd taken twelve photographs of Home Run—sleeping, eating, jumping for a Frisbee, running with a stick, and so on.

"Isn't he a *natural*?" Stewart asked, watching my face as I looked through the snapshots.

"He really is cute," I said.

"He's well-trained and everything. Look at him there—he can jump about six feet off the ground; I'm not kidding."

"He's a darling." I started to return the pictures to Stewart, but he told me to hang on to them for a while.

"Maybe when you're down in New York filming another commercial, you could show the pictures around. I mean, don't you think he'd make a fantastic TV star?"

Now, instead of breath mints, Mom was handing me throat lozenges. We were sitting in the waiting room of the Monaco Casting Agency, and for once there were very few people waiting with us. Two girls my age and their mothers were just leaving as we arrived, and two mother-type actresses were chatting in another corner.

My head was hurting, and I was worried that by the time I got to say my lines my throat would have closed completely and all I'd get out was a croak. I was also moping about school and the kids and Stewart, and suddenly the door opened and it was as if someone had turned on a solar switch. All my troubles melted into nothing, on the spot.

"Heather!"

She was in a pink raincoat and a matching rainhat and really did look the way Mom described her, like some sort of dewy flower someone had just plucked out of a garden.

Her face had cleared up (not quite, she said, but I could hardly see the eruption under her lip she was worrying about), and the wet weather was helping the ripples in her hair, which looked even more shiny and golden—if that was possible.

"Sunday!" We had a spectacular reunion; our mothers even hugged and kissed as if they'd just met after a separation of ten years.

We did a lot of chatting and laughing together while we waited to be called inside, and it turned out that Heather was seriously being considered for this commercial, too—for the part of a girl who sat on her blanket patting on Coco Balm lotion and looking tanned and unburned. Her line was, "I used to burn until I found Coco Balm. Now I just tan. My problem is, I still can't play volleyball!"

Luckily, we weren't in competition, so we really meant it when we wished each other good luck for the audition. Wouldn't it be fantastic, we said, if we *both* got to go to Florida?

I'd started out that morning feeling sick and awful but wound up feeling really top-of-the-world. "See what two aspirins can do!" Mom kidded later, when all four of us were sitting in a little restaurant together, having lunch. It was really like a party, because Heather and I felt we'd both performed pretty well, that our looks enhanced each other, and that the lady and two men in charge of making this casting choice had been in a huddle long enough to give us the impression that we might be the lucky two.

"You should have seen Sunday throw her head back and speak those lines as if they were Shakespeare!" Heather said, and I told everybody that only Heather could have pouted in that cute way when she said she couldn't play volleyball.

And then we said it together, just as if it were another line we'd rehearsed for a week. "We were dynamite!" and we all laughed so loud everyone around us turned to see what was so funny.

It happened so fast I didn't even have time to worry that someone else might have gotten the part after all.

The day after our audition I was home in bed with the worst cold of my life (into which the scratchy throat had now turned) when the telephone rang. It caught Mom just as she was about to stick the thermometer into my mouth, and although she managed to do it before running off to pick it up on the third ring, she practically jumped a foot.

It was the first time a decision had come so fast, and it was Mr. Farley himself who called. Of course, all I heard was Mom's side of the conversation. She kept saying, "That's wonderful news, wonderful!" and sort of laughed as if there were someone in the room with her, tickling her under the chin. "Wait until I tell her" is another thing I heard her say. "She'll be thrilled!"

A few minutes later she was back at the side of my bed. She pulled out the thermometer so I could speak.

"What did he say?" I yelped.

"They loved your long braid."

"That's *all*?"

"And"—Mom let out a whoop—"we leave a week from today for Boca Raton. We're flying Air Florida. We get two free nights at the Boca Inn and as much Coco Balm suntan oil as we need to sit in the sun for three glorious days!"

"I can't believe it," I said at least five times.

Mom actually did a little spin around the foot of the bed. I imagined it was the kind of thing she used to do on ice skates.

And she'd saved the best news for last. They'd chosen Heather for the other part, so we'd all be going together.

This time it was Mom who said it. "It certainly is dynamite news!" She was waving the thermometer as if it were a baton.

"Mom, do I have a temperature?"

Mom laughed and said, "You know, I forgot to look!" and she squinted so she could read the little numbers in the glass without her glasses. "A very slight temperature. Very slight."

"That's what you think!" I laughed.

15

ALTHOUGH I don't think I have any magic powers, my cold disappeared in two more days. I really willed it to be gone. At a time like this, I could not be in bed eating soup and blowing my nose. Of course, I took the extra time to try to study (if only my mind would stay on Orion's Sword, Reticulum, Corona Australis, instead of bathing suits, plane tickets, and luggage), but it was as if I were already buckled into the seat aboard a 747, and when I finally took The Whip's retest I had the feeling it wasn't going to get a much higher grade than the first one.

I don't know how many telephone conversations I had with Heather the week before we left, but there were endless things to discuss, and the kids at school, even Karen, didn't want to hear me worrying about whether last year's shorts were going to fit or whether the film in my camera was going to be ruined by the security X-ray at the airport. In fact, all they could talk about was the success of the white elephant sale, which had netted over eight hundred dollars, including the one hundred and fifty someone had paid for the vermeil picture frame. It was considered the greatest fund-raising event in the history of the school.

It's not that I wasn't interested in my school or my friends' activities, but when I yawned, what it meant was that I'd stayed up late studying or was tired from running up in the attic trying to find my sandals or helping Mom with summer-clothes laundry. I guess the kids didn't see it that way, because on the day before I left I got the message—the hard way.

I always seem to be on the verge of being late for phys. ed., because the gym is down a flight of stairs and all the way across the building from math class, so I never have enough time to change from my regular clothes into gym clothes. It's the reason I never bother to lock my locker, because the combination lock takes forever to open and I only keep my old beat-up sneakers and shorts and a t-shirt in there anyway.

That day, as usual, I came rushing down from math. I flung open the locker door and found absolutely nothing unusual inside, nothing that would tip me off to the nasty surprise someone had cooked up for me.

I took off my sweater and skirt and jumped into my

shorts and t-shirt, and then I took off my shoes and stuck my feet into my sneakers the way I've done a thousand times.

Squish.

Something was wet and cold and awful inside, oozing right through my socks and creeping between my toes. Yukk. I quickly yanked off my sneakers and looked inside. They were gloppy with some icky white goo and so were my wet and soggy feet, my socks, shoelaces, and now, my fingers. I recognized the smell. Wintermint Toothpaste.

"What is that?" Holly Knapp was staring at me. She happened to be standing at her locker, which is next to mine, and obviously she had had no part in this. I wasn't sure about any of the other girls in our locker aisle, though. They all came running to view me, the mucky laughing-stock, and some of them exchanged knowing glances even while they were saying, "Oh, how mean!" and "Who could have done such a terrible thing to you?" I even heard a snicker, but I guess I'll never know from whom.

I suddenly could feel it coming over me, like another cold, like one of those awful sneezes that practically shakes you top to bottom. Although I try to be a great sport, I guess I'm not a very good joke-butt; I didn't want to laugh and pretend it was all great fun. I wanted to cry. I wanted to burst right out, let tears fly, maybe even sob. They all couldn't have been in on it, but it seemed that way— the Stanhope Junior High girls versus me.

But I silently reminded myself to "smile if it *kills* you!"

I'd pulled it off in the cafeteria when they'd stuck dog bones into my lunchbag. Even if this was much more embarrassing, awful, nasty, I had to keep up the good front. "Very funny," I said, staying as cool as I was sure Heather would have stayed under the circumstances, and I turned to all the girls who were standing there waiting for me to fall apart or scream or throw one of the soggy sneakers against the wall. "At least I'm pretty sure of one thing," I said. "I won't be getting any cavities in my toes!" And I felt very proud of myself for coming up with a comeback to save a little—but not very much—face.

Karen had heard about the whole episode by lunchtime (news travels faster than smoke at our school), so I didn't have to tell her. "Some girls are jealous," she told me. "And it's true some people think you're a snob. It's only because they don't know you, Sun."

"I can't believe kids could be so mean," I said. "Do you think kids think I'm bragging when I talk about my auditions?"

"Well, sometimes it does come across that way."

"I'll never mention anything about my work again!"

"Then they'll think you're being snobby and secretive."

"I can't win!"

"Some kids will always envy you. I guess it's better just not to take it seriously."

"It's hard to smile when you've got toothpaste up to your ankles. And by the way, I got a late demerit in gym. Miss Dodd wouldn't listen when I tried to explain why I

131

was late *and* sneakerless. She said, 'You've been late once too often, Donaldson,' in her killer voice."

"Better just to forget it, Sun. Here, have half of my peanut butter on hard muffin. Mom worked late and didn't have time to go to the market. That's all we had in the house. And you think you've got problems!"

"You're right. By the time I get to the beach in Florida tomorrow, I'll bet it'll be right out of my mind," I said, but we both knew that even if I lived long enough to see my braid turn silver gray and old enough to do commercials for denture cream, I'd never forget today in the locker room.

It was the day of departure, and my collarbone was throbbing. According to my bedside clock, it was four-fifteen, and I'd already been up once at two and once at about three. Now I was more than excited; I was worried. If it was sleeting or snowing, would the airport close? Would our flight be delayed? If we were grounded, would the Coco Balm people hire some Florida kid to fill in for me? It seemed incredible that they were paying Mom's and my fare when there was a whole state of kids down there to choose from. Mom said that they'd rather choose kids they know are professional (!), and many Florida kids talk with a Southern accent and might sound funny up north or out west. Finding a girl like me isn't easy, Mom said, but I wasn't so sure. It seemed the world was full of red-hot competition.

I must have put in two more hours of tossing and turning. What if Dad's car was snowed into the garage and he couldn't get us to the airport? What if Mrs. Mlcik decided she couldn't baby-sit for Edward? What if the plane went up in the bad weather and then crashed into the ocean twenty minutes later?

My alarm rang! Time to get up. I heard Mom and Dad in their room; they were up, too. I flew around like my feet were on fire. I washed my hair and blew it dry—Mom would braid it on the way to the airport, she said. I brushed my teeth and threw on the clothes I'd put out for the flight the night before. Not the ski sweater this time— I'd only have to take it off the minute we got into a southern climate. Mom thought a lighter weight sweater and a blazer would work if we put the heater on in the car on the way to the airport, even though the snow was really starting to come down.

Yet, it was a funny thing. I'd misplaced my wishbone earrings, and there was no time to look for them. It seemed an omen. At the last minute, I reached for the sweater that had brought me so much luck and I thought: I hate to leave you *and* the earrings behind. I had a strange sense of foreboding. If I had to do it again, I would have put it on, even if it did seem wrong for Boca Raton. Maybe I might have warded off the bad luck that seemed to settle over the whole Coco Balm project like the lowering dark sky that greeted us as we stepped off the plane in Florida.

16

THE Florida rain was falling in heavy sheets just the way it does up north in winter, but at least, as Mom kept saying, there was no snow.

We'd left New York just as it began to fall heavily there, but all my worries were for nothing—Mrs. Mlcik arrived early and there was no delay at the airport. Even though the runway was already white as the plane took off, we didn't crash or even wobble, just lifted right up and up until we were well above snow and clouds, in a sort of hazy-blue nothing above the world.

But as Mom and I stepped into the glossy lobby of the Boca Inn that afternoon, my disappointment gave way to awe. It was ultra-glamorous, with huge sofas, chandeliers, and floor-to-ceiling glass windows that looked out onto a swimming pool practically the size of the school cafeteria, with a litte bridge over its middle, and a twisted slide running into it at one end. Beyond that was the beach, without the palm trees I'd expected. The palm trees were right here, in the lobby!

And our room! It had two double beds—I got one all to myself, the one facing the color TV set with a screen practically double the size of the one we have in our den at home. In fact, the room was so big I imagined it had been intended for six or seven sleepers instead of just two.

Of course, I wanted to call Heather right away, but Mom thought it would be wise to unpack first, and look around downstairs a bit; maybe we'd run into her in the coffee shop instead of disturbing her the minute we both arrived.

But we didn't run into her in the coffee shop. We ran into one of the ladies we'd met at the Monaco Casting Agency, who introduced us to the producer of the commercial, Mr. Jaffe. Mr. Jaffe told us that the weather was supposed to clear up within four hours, and although it would certainly be too late to start filming today, we'd get a very early start on the beach in the morning. He told me to get a good night's rest so I wouldn't have any circles under my eyes. "See you on the beach first thing in the morning, Beautiful!" he said cheerfully when we left the coffee shop.

Only, when I woke up the next morning, there was no sun.

The rain, which was supposed to have stopped the day before, was still beating on our big windows when I woke up at seven, and the beach looked not golden-white, but like a long strip of dirty wet rug rolling into dark water.

I'd called Heather the night before but never got to talk to her; her mother said she'd fallen asleep early and would see me at the shoot first thing. When the phone rang at eight I was sure it was Heather and jumped right up, but it was Mr. Jaffe. He sounded as glum as the weather and told us to do whatever we liked, but please not to leave the hotel in case it suddenly cleared up. He said it was supposed to be sunny by late morning.

Mom thought it would be best not to call Heather's room too early, so we went down to breakfast and ate steak and eggs with the cameraman and two other members of the technical crew. (I promised myself that I would not brag about steak at breakfast at school, no matter what.) I also kept looking at the door, expecting to see Heather appear every time it opened.

After breakfast, as we stopped at the newsstand to buy Mom a newspaper, we did run into her mother, though. "Where's Heather?" I asked immediately.

Mrs. Burstein was busy looking over different newspapers, trying to decide which one to buy, and seemed more interested in making the right choice than in answering my question.

"She's decided to stay up in our room for the day. She's not feeling one hundred percent," she said.

"Why, what's wrong?" I asked, but I didn't get much

of an answer. I did get a little poke from my own mother, signaling me not to ask too many questions. Mom doesn't like me to be too nosy. Heather's mom paid for her paper and left, and I didn't see her again for the rest of the day.

The rain continued. Mom and I spent the day looking in the hotel boutique, doing a crossword puzzle, reciting my lines, watching weather reports on television (eight inches of snow in Connecticut! I wondered if they'd closed the schools), watching Mr. Jaffe pace to the windows and smoke cigarettes, and chatting with the actress who was going to play the part of my mother and a few other members of our crew. Late in the afternoon, while Mom had gone upstairs to call home, one of the bellhops came over to me. I'd seen him looking at me now and again during the day.

"I've seen you on TV, haven't I?" he asked. "I recognize the braid."

"I've done a few commercials," I answered, and tried not to act too thrilled, but it was the first time I'd ever been recognized.

"I know I've seen you. Flipping pancakes, right?"

"No, toothpaste. Wintermint. I also had a very small part in a dog-food commercial."

"Oh, yeah! Right! Now I remember! Squeezing toothpaste! It's the first time I've ever met a real TV performer. You know, you really look even better in person!"

137

Wow. My first fan, and no Heather to tell the story to. Was she really sick? Mom stayed firm about my not calling her although I worked hard to wear her down. She'd come back from calling home, saying it was hard to understand Mrs. Mlcik, but that she'd said the snow had stopped, and although they'd been without power during the night, now it was back on. Yes, the schools were closed. At least, that's what Mom *thought* Mrs. Mlcik was saying.

"I wonder what the kids are doing," I said, thinking aloud.

"Well, if you really want company, there's someone your age over there." Mom pointed to a streaky-haired girl sitting near one of the palm trees across the lobby.

Mom thinks it's okay to go over to any stranger who looks my age and start a conversation—out of the blue (or gray) sky. She thinks anyone of my general size and shape can become an instant friend. "Mom, see that lady over there? She looks about your age—want to go talk to her?"

Mom did not think that was funny and she didn't laugh, but last week she'd heard me say, "We'll have the time of our lives" to Heather on the phone, and "I can't wait," and "Won't it be fun?" and she knew how disappointed I was. And now, really worried. "You made your point," she said, "but I still don't want you to call Heather's room. It may really disturb her if she's not feeling well."

"Okay, you've made *your* point, Mom. And I'm sorry. I

didn't mean to be fresh, but I've never seen so many dark clouds in my life! I just wish it would clear up."

I got my wish. Sunshine at last. We woke up to a sky filled with it, water reflecting it, a beach glowing gold, surf foaming white—the world looked as if it had just come out of the laundry! I jumped into my bathing suit and Mom helped blow-dry my hair; she braided it twice before she felt she'd gotten it perfect, even though the hairdresser would probably rebraid it, and we went downstairs. We'd been told to gather in the lobby at eight sharp if the sun was out, and although we arrived not more than three minutes after eight, it looked as if everyone was already there. Everyone, that is, except Heather or her mother.

The mood seemed so different today. The producer was wearing denim cut-offs, and almost everyone else was in bathing suits or shorts. Half the group seemed to be wearing t-shirts with a "Jaffe Productions" logo. Some people had straw hats. Could this really be a working day?

We got our instructions. Outside, at poolside, we would find a breakfast buffet. I could see it from the lobby, a long table of food that looked even more feastlike than Jonathan Levy's Bar Mitzvah, to which practically the whole of Stanhope Junior High had been invited last fall. No swimming until later, please, Mr. Jaffe said. He hoped we would be able to finish shooting very early, so we could spend at least part of the afternoon on the beach. If not, there was still tomorrow morning, and if any of us wanted to stay until late tomorrow afternoon, arrangements could be made. He passed out about a hundred tubes of Coco Balm and said, "Grease up, everybody!"

Still, no Heather. Outside, at the buffet, as I heaped my plate with pineapple and melon and a Danish shaped like a figure eight, I kept looking for her. My appetite surprised me. It wasn't long ago I couldn't even get down a bite of a doughnut before filming. I must really be getting to be a pro!

And then I spotted her under a straw hat, wearing dark glasses. She and her mother appeared at the glass doors leading out to the pool from the hotel. She was in a white bathing suit with red trim and looked as if a spotlight had been beamed right at her. I waved like crazy, and she waved back, but she didn't come running, the way I would have. She just kept her steady, slow pace, cool as ever.

"Your bathing suit is dynamite!" I called over as soon as she was close enough for me to really see it. Now I could see that the red trim was really a row of red hearts, and I immediately wished mine weren't just a boring blue-and-green-striped racing number. The wardrobe lady had said, "Keep it simple," but maybe I should run upstairs and put on the yellow one with the white daisies anyway?

"Your braid has gotten so long!" Heather said, coming up close, and then I looked at her face and I blinked. I had to look again to make sure I hadn't imagined what I saw.

In the strong sunlight, despite her dark glasses, despite the shade of the straw hat, nobody could miss it. There were big red pimples on her chin, one that looked almost big enough to be a bee or wasp sting, two or three big eruptions clustered over her eyebrows, and even though her cheeks were pretty clear, her face looked almost as if she'd broken out in a rash. Poor Heather. Even though I tried to keep it from showing, I suppose my eyes just bugged out with shock.

"It's okay," she said. "Bad luck I broke out just before we were set to leave—and then they got worse down here yesterday, but I'm pretty sure we can cover everything with stage makeup. I don't think they intend to do any real closeups of me anyway."

"Heather, what about the super doctor in New York you've been going to?"

"Mom took me down last week, and he said I just turned out to be more difficult to treat than he thought. He put me under this special lamp and he's given me stronger stuff, but it takes a week or two to be effective."

"It'll be all right, honey," Heather's mother said, giving Heather's shoulder a pat. She'd come up behind us. "I know makeup will cover it," she said, but although her mouth was fixed in a smile, it seemed more show business than real, like the kind of grin you work up when someone is about to snap your picture.

* * *

"Okay, everybody, down to the beach!" Mr. Jaffe waved us away from the buffet in the direction of the camera crew and the technical people, who had already set up beach towels, sun-umbrella, the silks (big white trampoline-type awnings that cut glare from the sun), a volleyball net, and all the stuff needed to shoot the commercial.

Mom wished me luck and gave me a sort of wink when the hairdresser came to rebraid my hair, and then she moved off to sit in a folding chair and do another crossword puzzle. As she was leaving, she whispered, "I wonder if Mr. Jaffe has seen poor Heather's face," and not a minute later, the makeup lady arrived. She gave my braid a sort of a tug and said, "It's going to be long enough to sit on pretty soon! We'll do your makeup over there, under that umbrella. We're going to paint you the color of sunburn, and we're going to leave a white stripe down your back, as if the braid has protected you in that spot. When they lift the braid in the commercial, it'll show the contrast and be really effective. Hey!"

I spun around to see what had caught her attention and realized Heather and her mother had joined us.

"Honey! What happened to your face?" The makeup lady's name was Bitsy, or at least that's what everyone called her because she was so small, but her voice was very big, and I was so embarrassed for Heather I wanted to duck under the nearest beach towel and disappear.

"I'm sure your makeup will cover that, won't it?"

142

Heather's mom asked. She tried to keep her sort-of smile going but wasn't doing any better with it than Heather was. In fact, Heather looked as if she'd just been bitten by a sand crab.

"No way! Are you kidding? We can do a lot with grease-paint, but I have nothing that will cover ee-ruptions like those!"

I could practically feel Heather cringe.

"But at least you can try, can't you?"

"Listen, Mrs. Burstein, I've been doing this for six years, and I guess I know what'll work and what won't work."

"But won't you please, please just . . . try?"

I tried not to look at Heather, who now seemed to have focused on some little spot down at the far end of the beach—maybe the jetty, which seemed like just a row of pebbles from here and certainly not that interesting. It's as if she weren't listening at all, had left her face and body here, but packed up her heart and mind and soul and had taken off.

I remember how I'd felt when Gray Beard had called me awkward, and now I felt like throwing my arms around Heather and telling her it didn't mean a thing, but it would have come out sounding fake. To Heather's heart and mind and soul, it meant everything.

"She's all broken out. I don't think it's smart to touch her face," Bitsy said. Although she didn't look that old, I guessed that Bitsy had never been a kid and had never had a zit.

Heather's mother was squeezing her pocketbook. I watched the little threads of perspiration form right above her lipstick, and in a way I was sorry Mom was busy with her puzzle, out of earshot. Maybe she could have helped talk Bitsy into trying to fix Heather's complexion, or at least could have told her to keep her voice down. Everyone seemed to be looking in our direction.

"Impossible," Bitsy said.

"Please—" Mrs. Burstein pleaded.

"Mr. Jaffe!" Bitsy waved and called until she caught the producer's attention.

He was busy looking through the camera viewfinder and didn't immediately catch sight of Bitsy. When he finally came over I saw that he was perspiring, too, and his t-shirt was stuck to his chest in a stripe along the front. "What's up?" he asked.

"Look at this," Bitsy said, pointing to Heather as if she were a *this* instead of a person.

I couldn't see Mr. Jaffe's eyes behind his dark glasses either, but I could see his mouth. He stretched it across his teeth as if he had just bitten into something very cold. "Oh, . . . ," he said. I'm not allowed to use the word he used. "When the . . . did that happen, Heather?"

Mrs. Burstein said, "She's being treated for it, Mr. Jaffe. It's just a temporary little outbreak, and I've been telling Bitsy here I think we could hide it with makeup. Don't you think so?" She was talking very fast, and I noticed she'd moved closer and was about to touch Mr. Jaffe's

144

arm, but he moved away, took a quick step to one side, and acted as if she weren't there at all. Then for a split second I thought she looked as if she were going to sink right down into the sand on her knees. "Please—" she said.

Heather was terrific. She didn't change her expression one bit. She didn't look as if she would double over or scream or burst out in a loud wail the way any ordinary kid might have. "It's all right. It's sort of been coming the last few days," she said, staying very dignified, as if she were talking about how her rose garden was coming along, instead of a horrible case of acne.

Mr. Jaffe suddenly seemed to remember he was talking to a person with feelings instead of a doorstop. "Well, I hate to say this, honey, but I just can't use you in this spot, sweetheart. I'm sorry. I'm really sorry, doll. It's just one of those things. We can't hide a skin condition like that. Don't feel bad, okay? I just can't *do* it." He turned and waved his arm at the director, who was arranging a big bottle of Coco Balm on a lounge chair. "Harry! You're not gonna believe this, but we got a little problem here." He tore off his sunglasses, wiped his forehead off with the back of his arm, and yelled, "How long do you think it'll take to get the backup out here on the beach?"

17

IT was four-thirty. I remember the exact time because I'd just asked Mom how much longer the sun would stay up in the sky. We had finished filming about twenty minutes before. I'd washed off the sunburn makeup, rushed up to the pool to see if I could find Heather there, and now I was back at the beach looking up and down for her. We still had at least two more hours to enjoy the day together, and I knew she and her mother hadn't left because I'd seen Mrs. Burstein sitting not far from Mom the whole time we were filming.

It had gone pretty smoothly, and Heather's replacement, the girl with the streaky hair I'd seen in the lobby the day before, Tara, spoke her lines very clearly and without a southern accent, even though she was a Florida girl. I did intend to tell Heather that Tara could definitely not give the performance the same *zing*, though.

If I could find Heather.

I went up to her room and knocked on her door. No answer. Luckily, I found her mother sitting in the lobby. She was sitting near the windows but seemed to be staring at nothing, although there was a magazine open on her lap. "I've had enough sun," she said, looking as if she meant, "I've had enough *everything*."

"Where's Heather, Mrs. Burstein?" I asked. "I've been all over looking for her."

"Up in our room. She said she preferred staying up there to read because the beach was too windy." Mrs. Burstein shrugged and added, "She just wanted to be alone, I guess."

"She's not up there." I told her I'd knocked on the door about four times without getting an answer.

"She might have fallen asleep. I'd better go up and wake her. If she sleeps now she'll be up all night. I think we made a mistake staying on here, but our room is paid for and I thought Heather would enjoy getting a little sun before we have to go back to the snow. I didn't expect her to take being replaced this hard."

"Shall I go up and wake her?"

"Would you, Sunday? And, could you talk to her? Tell her this commercial isn't important? It's nothing! She'll get other parts. Her father and I have a lot of connections in the city, and in a few weeks, when she gets back her peaches-and-cream complexion, we'll really get things moving! In fact, I've just heard they're casting a new

Broadway musical about a Pilgrim family, and they're looking for a twelve-year-old to play the second lead." Mrs. Burstein was digging in her straw pocketbook and finally fished out her room key. "And Heather can still pass for eleven or twelve, don't you think, Sunday?"

I said I thought so, and I took the key and went straight back up to the Bursteins' room.

It was an exact duplicate of ours except the wallpaper was blue and white instead of green and white, and there was a seagull picture hanging over each of the beds (ours had seashells). I knew which bed was Heather's, too, not only because it was messed up, but because she'd left her straw hat, sunglasses, and book on the wrinkled bedspread. "Heather?" I called a couple of times, which was pretty stupid, because I could see the whole room and even into the bathroom, which was empty, and unless she was hiding in a closet or under a bed, it was obvious she was not there.

When I told Mrs. Burstein, she said she thought Heather might have gotten bored and gone to the coffee shop for a soda or might be browsing in the little gift shop on the lower level of the hotel.

I said I'd keep looking until I found her.

But she wasn't in the coffee shop, and she wasn't down in the gift shop, either. Instead of going back and bothering Mrs. Burstein again, I decided she must be somewhere on the beach. Earlier, the waterfront had been pretty crowded (we'd gathered quite a bunch of onlookers when we were filming), and it was hard to find anyone unless they were smack in front of you, but now the crowd had definitely thinned and I could see pretty far to the left and down the beach to the right all the way to the jetty. Swimmers were allowed only in certain areas roped off in front of the lifeguards, and there seemed to be very few people in the water now, so I focused on any white-and-red bathing suit as far as my eye could see. I did see one very far down to the right, under an umbrella, but when I looked again I saw that it was someone picking up a baby, someone older, with dark hair, who looked nothing like Heather at all.

And then, in the direction of the jetty, I saw another figure in a white suit with red trim and I was dead sure it was Heather, just sitting alone on the sand, right at the water's edge, knees up, staring out at the surf. Her hair was the right color, but it was pinned up, and I'd never seen Heather's hair any other way but flowing to her shoulders, so I couldn't be sure, but if she'd been swimming, wouldn't she have pinned it up? Yes, it must be Heather! I broke into a sprint.

It felt wonderful to run, to weave in and out between the blankets and the umbrellas to the music coming from portable radios, feel the hot sand under my feet and the sun on my shoulders. I'd get Heather to jump the waves with me—they really looked high and cold and just menacing enough to give us a real thrill. This is what I'd dreamed about in cold Connecticut for so many weeks.

I'd cheer Heather right up. Who could be unhappy riding in on a wave?

As I got closer to the girl with the pinned-up hair, a big guy with muscles like a boxer came bounding out of the water. He stood in front of her and sprinkled her with water, and she jumped up and ran away from him, laughing. Why had I thought this was Heather? Her bathing suit was white, but the trim I'd seen as red was fuscia pink, and this person was much older, taller, and heavier.

And then something caught my eye. It wasn't white or red; it was pink. Pink as bubble gum, pink as a baby's blanket, pink as Heather's raincoat. It was moving slowly along the jetty—heading out.

Could it be Heather, on the *jetty*?

"Heather! Heather!" Of course, she was much too far out to hear me. "HEATHER!"

I'd started running toward the jetty, not sure I wasn't making another stupid mistake. I'd probably run along the rocks screaming my head off only to have some fisherman in a pink shirt turn around and tell me to stop scaring off the fish.

"Heather!" I had to be careful. The rocks looked so slippery they might have been oiled, and out here the water wasn't fooling around. It was inky, it was deep, and there was probably an undertow. No one else had ventured out this far, either. The lifeguard's chair looked the size of a matchbook from here.

"Heather!" She kept walking, if it was Heather. I followed. Now I saw the hair, and it was no fisherman. Heather! It's me, Sunday!" I screamed at her two more times before she heard me.

She turned, looked, and then, instead of stopping and waiting for me, she turned right back around and kept walking. I couldn't believe it. It was Heather for sure. She'd looked right at me, and it was as if her eyes weren't working and she hadn't seen me at all.

I stopped following her. To tell the truth, I wasn't anxious to go out any farther. What if I slipped off the rocks? I can swim well enough, but the undertow out here looked even more evil than the current close to the shore, and we all knew that even pretty shallow water could sweep you just where it wanted to—out to France or straight under to Australia—before you could even let out a scream for help. I was pretty much out of breath, too, so I stopped calling, not that she could hear me now anyway. She'd made her way along the rocks and was almost out to the end of the jetty, a little pink figure no bigger than a begonia, wobbling along by herself.

Not that I'd just leave her out there, of course. I intended to run like the dickens, straight to the lifeguard, and tell him to get her to come back. "She's out there, at the end of the jetty," I was sort of silently rehearsing what I'd say, "and I don't think it's safe! I tried to call her back, but she ignored me, just kept moving. You can't miss her—she's wearing a pink raincoat."

Pink raincoat. Waitaminute. It was hotter than anything now, the sun was up there still blazing away as if to make up for two days of playing hookey, and Heather was wearing a raincoat. I imagined the lifeguard's face, a big question mark. "Why would anyone wear a raincoat in this weather?" He might well ask.

And in a flash as cold as the murky water that was lapping at the mossy rocks all around me, it hit me. Virginia Woolf!

There was no time to go back to get the lifeguard. "Heather! Heather!" I screamed until my throat felt like I'd sandpapered it, and when she wouldn't turn, wouldn't answer, I moved ahead along the rocks, half-crouching, moving along, sometimes practically on all fours, watching my step but going as quickly as I could. I slipped once and my heart went absolutely so wild I thought that if kids could have heart attacks, my time might have come. I saw myself plunging headlong into the ocean, trying to cling to the slimy rocks, but being swirled away like soap-suds down a drain.

"Heatherheatherheather!" I shrieked. It seemed to take forever, but I was finally not far behind her, so she had to turn to look at me. I think I'd surprised her by coming all the way out here, where probably only brave fishermen or dangerous electric eels had ever braved the rocks.

Her face looked even worse than it had this morning, because now her eyes were red, too, probably from crying, and her nose was the color of her raincoat.

"What are you doing here!" I screamed at her. Not in any horror movie I've ever seen in my life have I been as scared as I was then. I knew exactly what was in her mind. And I knew exactly what was in the pockets of her pink raincoat.

Rocks.

I was panting, scared crazy, and felt as if some switch in my body had been turned to On. Everything was pumping, beating, and pulsing like machinery under my bathing suit.

"Give it to me!" I yelled. "Hand it over!" I shrieked. I meant the raincoat. I saw the big bulging pockets, and I must have screamed like a maniac. I think Heather really got scared. When she hesitated, I lunged at her, holding her shoulders, sure we would both go sailing off the rocks together. I tore the coat open, thanking God for snaps instead of buttons, and the rest was easy. She just stood there shaking, letting me pull it off her shoulders. All the time I was screaming, "Why would you do that? What made you do something so *dumb*? Do you realize what you almost *did*?"

I don't know what sort of weightlifter strength got into me, but I must say Stewart would have been proud of me. I hurled the raincoat the way he pitches a hardball. It went flying and then it fell, a rock-heavy deadweight that hit the water with a splash and went under in less time than it would take to say, "Transition."

Together, Heather and I watched it disappear.

* * *

"I wasn't going to jump," Heather said, as we were walking along the rocks heading back to the beach.

I couldn't answer. My throat was too sore, my heart was too sore. Even my feet were hurting.

"It's not that show business is that important to me," she went on. "See, it's my mother and my father. It's family tradition, and it's not that they'd come right out and *say* I was a failure. It's just that every time they looked at me, I could feel how *they* felt—that I was *letting* my skin break out, not *trying* hard enough. They'd put all this effort into me, all this money, all this work, and I was turning into a *loser*. I was letting them down."

"Heather, you're not a loser!"

"I wasn't going to jump in, Sunday. I honestly wasn't. I just figured, though, that if I slipped and fell, well, then it was okay with me. It was out of my hands. Do you know what I mean?"

I pictured the raincoat in the water, the sleeves all filled out as if there were still arms in them, the way it had vanished in a second, leaving just a frill of bubbles on the surface, and it was as if someone had put a bunch of cold seaweed at the back of my neck. "When you get back to the hotel, promise you'll get rid of that book. Promise me, Heather," I said, when my sore voice came back.

She was quiet for a long time. "I will if you promise never to tell anyone what happened today," she finally said, and then something between us just snapped shut, and as we walked together along the beach, she turned back into the cool, distant girl I'd first seen in the Farley Agency waiting room.

All the way back to the hotel, neither of us said another word.

18

I NEVER saw Heather again.

Of course, I saw her pouring Sweet Vermont Maple Syrup on a waffle, jumping in Grid-Kid sneakers, and playing with Johnny-Up Magic Dice, but those were old commercials, made the year before or the year before that, and whenever they appeared on our television screen I felt like running right out of the room.

When Mom and I went to the Pilgrim musical tryouts for a "cattle call" the week after we got home, although at least three hundred girls showed up and I kept looking through the crowd for the long, blonde hair, neither Heather nor her mother was there.

I thought about her a lot. I thought about her during the day and dreamed about her at night, and once or twice, a few days after we got back from Florida, I almost called her to tell her that now I was beginning to understand how she felt.

Coming home on the plane, Mom kept asking me why I was so quiet. Was I tired? Didn't I feel well? Had the trip been too exhausting? A disappointment? Luckily, when the stewardess came to take our drink order, she recognized me. "Haven't you done some TV commercials?" she asked. "I know I've seen you!" Mom was absolutely tickled pink. I'd told her about the bellhop, but this time she saw it for herself, how people light right up when they think they've seen you on their television screens.

The stewardess wanted to know how long it took to grow my braid that long, and how old I was, and how I'd gotten my start. She said she'd always wanted to do exactly what I was doing and might give up flying next year just to give it a try. After she'd served us dinner, she came back again to ask Mom a million questions, and Mom was really pleased. I was glad, too, because it took me off the hook, having to explain why I wasn't my usual, happy self.

Then, at the airport, it happened again as we were waiting for our suitcases to arrive on the luggage carousel. An old lady with a shopping bag on each arm gave Mom's sleeve a tug. Her English wasn't too good, but we both understood what she was saying. She pulled at her own little gray wisps of hair to signal that she recognized my braid, and she told my mother I was a "nice girl. *Bonita!*"

Then she said, "TV. I seen her." And she nodded and smiled again and again, as if she were taking curtain calls.

Mom was grinning from ear to ear. "My daughter, the celebrity," she whispered to me when the old lady had moved away. "Doesn't it feel *good*, Sunday?"

"Yes," I said, and of course it did, but as we walked toward the exit, carrying our suitcases and the bag of oranges Mom was bringing home for Mrs. Mlcik, I wondered why it just didn't feel as good as I thought it would.

We got a surprise when we walked out of the luggage area into the terminal. Mom was going to see if she could find the airport limousine service instead of paying for a private taxi to take us back to Connecticut. She'd started to head for a sign that said GROUND TRANSPORTATION when, from out of nowhere, Dad appeared.

I was so happy to see him, I rushed right over to give him a hug and a kiss, but he warned me not to come too close. "I've got the most miserable cold," he said, "and I don't want you to catch it. At least, *you* look wonderful and healthy. How was Florida? Was it great?"

Mom was happy to see him, too, but as she was asking him if he was dressed warmly enough and why he hadn't put on his hat and what was he doing for his cough, I had the feeling that something worse than his cold was wrong with Dad.

I suppose it's the way Dad looked when he picked up

158

our suitcases, a little more tired, round-shouldered, and sad-looking. The cold didn't help, of course; his eyes were really red and watery, and his nose had that Easter-rabbit look, but usually, cold or no cold, Dad kids around and is talkative and lively, especially when we've been separated for a while.

"Well, how was it?" he asked when we got into the car, and that was a perfectly normal question, asked in a normal way. Still, something was hovering in Dad's voice that I didn't like.

Mom didn't catch it. She went on and on, about the hotel, how nice the production crew was, how lucky we'd arranged for a late flight so we could get a few more hours in the sun. "Did you come home early because of your cold?" she finally asked, and Dad shook his head.

He'd come home yesterday morning, he said, because when he called home the night before from New Jersey, to see how Edward and Mrs. Mlcik had weathered the snowstorm, Edward was crying.

"Edward—crying?" Mom's head swiveled on her neck as if it were going to make a full 360° turn. "Why was Edward *crying*?"

Suddenly Dad sneezed hard and blew his nose, and that seemed to make his anger spurt out as if it were another sneeze. "Because of his fish!"

"His fish? What about his *fish*?" Mom asked.

"The power failure!" Dad's voice was going high. "Half

of Stanhope was without power for eight hours. The snowstorm knocked out a major power line. You knew that, didn't you?"

"When I called, Mrs. Mlcik said the power was back on! Anyway, what does that have to do with Edward's *fish*?"

"Eight hours without light and heat! The house turned frigid. Of course, Edward and Mrs. Mlcik slept through most of it, but the water in the tank turned cold enough to kill off most of his fish. The poor kid—he fell apart. You've never seen anything like it. He took it so hard."

"Mrs. Mlcik didn't tell me!"

"I suppose she didn't want to ruin your trip."

"Poor Edward!" I said.

"I tried everything to cheer him up. I said I'd buy him new ones, but he said they wouldn't be the same. He's hardly left his room for two days. School was closed Thursday, but I actually had to force him to go today."

Mom was shaking her head. "I don't know what makes those fish so important to the boy."

"A few of them were just sort of half-alive for a few hours, and he tried this and that to save them, and then they died, one after another."

"The lion-fish? Did it die, too?" I asked. It was impossible to imagine Edward finding his fish floating dead at the top of the tank. I couldn't picture it.

"The big one you gave him?"

I nodded.

"I think so."

"I can't understand what it is he loves so about them," Mom said.

"They're like his . . . *family,*" Dad said, after a pause.

"His family! Oh, now really, Steve—" Mom protested, and then Dad sniffed and wiped his nose. Finally, he said, "I suppose his fish are substitutes for his real family, which is never really there for him."

Mom's voice changed. I know when she is gathering up what she calls "self-control," holding back words she doesn't want to say. "What do you mean 'Is never really there for him'? I'm always there."

"I think you only *seem* to be there, Shirl."

"*Seem* to be there?"

"And most of the time, I'm on the road, or feeling so wiped-out I hardly know what's going on in my own house."

"I don't know what you're saying. You *have* to travel. You have to earn a living. And half the mothers I know work, too. I don't work, I'm at home almost all the time, so you can't say I'm neglecting Edward."

Dad sneezed and I said, "Bless you," and even though Dad automatically said, "Thanks, Sun," it was as if they had both forgotten I was there, listening to every word.

"It seems as if every bit of energy has always gone to putting Sunday in the spotlight. From the time she was born. I went along with the superstar name, but we should have stopped short of the super effort, because it seems

161

to me that putting the spotlight on one kid can eclipse the other.

"Maybe I'm being too hard on us, Shirl, but when was the last time we actually *looked* at Edward? Or wanted to hear what he had to say or told him that even though he isn't on television, and he isn't adorable, we think *he's* a star, too?"

"Well, he's at an awkward stage right now. Of course, he'll grow out of it, but he's overweight and not too graceful, and he doesn't have too many friends. . . ."

"I think it's been easier for both of us to buy him chocolate bananas and doughnuts than to pay attention to him, don't you?"

Mom seemed upset and turned very silent. From my seat I could only see the back of her head except once in a while when she turned to look out of the side window. Then, even a quick glance at the side of her face made me uneasy. "Maybe you're right," is what she finally said, and her voice seemed watery, as if she'd caught Dad's cold.

I thought the subject was closed—until we got to the toll bridge. Then, while we were lined up behind about ten cars, Dad got a bout of sneezes and coughs and suddenly, out of nowhere, he said, "Half of it is my fault, of course."

He took a minute to put a cough drop in his mouth, and then he dropped what turned out to be a bombshell. He said his job was keeping him out of town too much, he was exhausted, miserable, and getting nowhere. He'd been thinking it over since our trip to Arizona. His father was getting ready to retire and could use someone to take over the business down there. Phoenix was a growth area, a great city; the weather was perfect; life would be a lot easier there for all of us. What did Mom think of leaving Connecticut and moving out west?

19

I MUST have slept that night, but it couldn't have been very much. I remember just staring at the wall of my room and watching scenes appear as if it were a television screen and someone were yelling, "Take One! Take Two!"

I saw Heather's raincoat, drowning again and again.

I saw Mrs. Burstein and Puddles O'Hanlon and Gray Beard and both my grandmothers.

I saw Mom and Dad sitting as far apart as they could in the front seat of the car. And through the wall, I heard them arguing what seemed like all night long, about moving, about Edward, about me.

"What happens to Sunday's career if we move to Arizona?"

"What happens to mine if we don't? Didn't you always say I ought to find a job that didn't demand my traveling so much?"

"Things are just opening up for her! Now is not the time to leave!"

"Are we going to sacrifice our family's future so Sunday can sell dog food on television?"

My mother was crying. *Crying!*

I thought about Uncle Walter and Aunt Cheryl and my little cousins, trying to smash Grandma's paperweight to get at the four-leaf clovers inside, and I thought about Karen's parents—her mother in Stanhope, her father in the city—and it was hard not to make a connection. I pictured Dad packing his big old suitcase, the one that still has his college stickers on it, and kissing us all good-bye. Then, no four-leaf clover would ever get us together again.

I couldn't get Edward's fish tank out of my mind, either.

Last night, when we came home, I passed it on my way upstairs, and it had only about four fish swimming around in its sort of ghostly green–lit water. The ceramic saguaro looked spooky and alone inside, and the plants were gray and grim.

Usually, Edward has to be screamed at to get in bed, but here it was, only six o'clock, and already he was under his covers half asleep. His first question whenever anyone gets back from anyplace is usually, "What'd ya bring me?" but instead, he sat up, holding himself up on his elbows, and asked if I'd heard about his fish. I told him I had. Did I know about Rex, he wanted to know. I told him I did and I was sorry.

"Dad couldn't bury them," Edward said. "Not even Scamp."

"Why not?"

"The ground was frozen solid. He just put them in a plastic bag and threw them in the garbage pail. Even Rex." Edward just blinked at me; he looked all cried out.

"Edward, I know how you feel."

"Naw, you don't," Edward said.

"I *do*," I insisted.

"Nobody does," Edward said, and he flopped back onto his pillow and pulled the sheet up to his nose.

"Good night, Edward," I said. "Don't feel bad."

He didn't answer.

I needed to talk to Karen so badly that I flew to the phone even before I'd unpacked my suitcase. I crossed my fingers, hoping this wasn't one of her weekends with her father, or that her line, which is always busy, wouldn't be busy.

Her mother picked up the telephone on the third ring. "We just saw you in the toothpaste commercial about five minutes ago! What a funny coincidence! How was Florida? Exciting, I bet! You are a lucky, lucky girl, Sunday. Everybody in town is talking about you!"

She put Karen on the phone. "You're back! How was it? Was it fabulous?"

"I've got so much to tell you, Karen! You'll never believe what happened—" I blurted.

"Oh, Sun, I'm dying to hear it. The only thing is, I'm so late! Erin is having this big party for all the kids who went out shoveling driveways after the snow—do you know we made over two hundred dollars the day they closed the schools? I think the school's actually reached its goal! Mrs. Beastly came on the intercom this morning and announced the sail is *on*!"

"That's wonderf—"

"Half of us are so sore we're going to take turns in Bim's parents' Jacuzzi tomorrow afternoon, but it was worth it! Guess what—Hiroshi asked me to go on the sail as his date, and I'm going. His English has really *improved*!"

"No kidd—"

"Listen, did you get a gorgeous tan? I'm dying to see it! Are you going to be in school Monday? I just don't have time to talk now, but I want to hear all about it! Say, did you hear we were without power for about eight hours? It was awesome!"

I must have fallen asleep a few times on and off during that night, but I remember waking up for good the next morning at about five. I felt something funny in my throat and imagined I'd caught my father's cold, but I was wrong. My throat was tight, my eyes were wet; it was my mother's crying I'd caught.

I wasn't surprised when The Whip called me to his desk after class Monday. I'd earned a failing grade for the marking period and was in danger of failing the course for the year. He said he was surprised and disappointed and also plenty mad, especially about the test on The Heavens: "Too many questions and not enough answers!" He hated to see a good student go pffft—down the drain. Why didn't I just wake up and shape up? Why didn't I get my priorities in order?

Why didn't I?

I thought about it all through lunch as I sat with my friends, who already seemed as out of reach as old yearbook photographs. I asked Karen if Stewart had been at Erin's party, and she nodded. I know Karen well enough to know there was something else she wasn't telling me, and sure enough, out of the corner of my eye, I saw Stewart take aim and throw his empty milk carton into a garbage pail about three tables away. A perfect, showoff shot. Showing off for whom? Then the paper from his straw went flying, and I followed its path through the air until it hit its intended target—Erin Wurtzel.

They were in their life and I was in mine. The kids would all have given their eyeteeth to be doing commercials like I was, and yet, here were another couple of questions without answers: Whose life was easier, more fun, better? Why did I feel as if I'd just had a perfect shot —wham—right to the heart?

"Remember when I first started doing commercials, you told me that if I wanted to quit, I would just be able to quit?" I asked Mom when I got home from school that same afternoon.

Mom was sitting in the kitchen with her feet up, drinking a cup of tea. She seemed thoughtful and quiet, not teary. I noticed a backgammon set open on the kitchen table, probably waiting for Edward to come downstairs and start taking an interest in board games.

"It's the Arizona business, isn't it?" she asked.

"It's everything."

"You don't have to give up your career, Sunday. I'm sure your father won't make us move. I think he was just upset because of Edward. You don't want to leave Stanhope, do you?"

"No. Well, I don't know. I love Stanhope, but I love Phoenix, too. I don't know *what* I want."

"You have a wonderful future in show business here. Of course, you can quit any time, but why, for heaven's sake, would you want to stop now?"

What could I say? Could I tell her it was because Edward's fish were dead or because of The Whip or because the kids had gone to a big party I'd missed? Could I tell her what I suspected about Stewart and Erin? Could I tell her about Heather's raincoat or about Karen having to eat Japanese food on Thanksgiving Day?

"We've got a frozen yogurt commitment this week and the Pilgrim musical auditions Friday. Why don't we give it just a little more time, honey? I hate to see you throw it all away!"

169

"I'm flunking science," I said.

"Well, it's no wonder. It's been too hectic these last few months. We've got to ease up a bit. Maybe you ought to spend next weekend in the library. I'll give you whatever help I can, Sunday. We may even hire a tutor; how would that be?"

I knew if I jumped up and said, "It's not what I thought it would be like! I want to stop now!" Mom would understand. She'd get right up and call Mr. Farley and tell him that I was too busy with schoolwork to continue my career, and that would be it.

But something held me back.

I know what it was. It was Mom's eyes. It was the way they could shine when someone called to congratulate her because they'd seen me on channel two or four or seven, the way they sparkled when the stewardess on the flight from Florida recognized me, the way they lit up when one of my grandmas was on the telephone and Mom would say, "Of course we're proud of her! She's fantastic!"

It was the way her eyes seemed now, as if the spotlight had gone out behind them and all her hopes for me had melted into the same gray slush we could see right out the kitchen window in our driveway.

Mom's ice skates were gone. It's as if I'd taken those away from her when I was born. I just didn't want to take anything more away from her now.

So I said, "I'd better go up and read up on The Heavens, then, study my French verbs. Better late than never.

And I'd better start reading *Catcher in the Rye*. Book report due in two weeks." Did I sound normal, ordinary, happy?

I guess so. Mom said, "Send Edward down when you go upstairs, will you, honey? I'm going to teach him backgammon. He'll probably get so good at it, he'll beat me by next week."

There was my problem: Mom loves us, tries hard, and wants us both to be happy. When I came home from school the very next day, there was a gift-wrapped box in the middle of the dining room table. It was the Bermuda bag I'd been dying for forever. In perfect blue.

"We'll get it monogrammed right away," Mom promised. She'd bought Edward a gift, too: a scrapbook and a big pair of grownup scissors. Dad was trying to get him interested in cutting pictures of sports stars out of the newspapers, the way *he* used to when he was a kid.

"Mom, it's not anybody's birthday. It's not Christmas." I don't know why I felt so guilty taking the bag.

"You've worked very hard. I think you deserve it," Mom said, and the big beautiful shine was right back there, lighting up her eyes.

20

AND so it went. I got the frozen yogurt job (but no part in the Pilgrim musical), spent most of my weekends catching up on the stuff I was missing in school during the week, and Mom and I stopped driving into the city and began taking the train so I could study on the way there and back. The hectic life continued, just as it had before.

Dad seemed to be home even less these days, and if Mom and Dad were arguing, they were doing it when I was asleep; most of the time all I heard between them was silence. Dad took Edward on a combination golf and business trip with him during spring vacation, and Edward came back thin. Well, thinner.

Then, around the beginning of May, it's as if my life exploded. The Coco Balm commercial and the frozen yogurt commercial were aired during the same week. On that Thursday, the local newspaper ran a picture of me that appeared on the first page of the second section with this headline: LOCAL TEENAGER HAS GLAMOROUS EXTRA-CURRICULAR CAREER. A reporter had interviewed me on the telephone, and the story came out saying I was "pert," "talented," and a "star of the future." It seemed as if every single person in Stanhope Junior High read it and ran over to congratulate me the next day. A lady who works in the cafeteria practically embarrassed me to death by coming over to our table at lunch and telling me I was a beautiful girl and that I looked just like her oldest daughter, Frieda. The custodian said "Congratulations," and the principal's secretary cut out the article and put it on the school bulletin board.

Even The Whip had seen the article. When I walked into science, he didn't say anything. He just stood up and began to applaud. Of course, all the other kids picked up on it, and Bim said, "And now, may I have the envelope please?" And then he said, "If you keep this up, they're going to name a day of the week after you." Everyone clapped and laughed for like five minutes until The Whip said, "When her grades go up, we can give her another round." Touché; I think my face turned purple.

When I was sitting in the library that Saturday a little kid handed me a slip of paper and a pen. I just looked at him because it never entered my head he could be asking for my autograph. "Would you sign it, please?" he asked, and when I did, about five of his little friends came running over from out of nowhere with *their* slips of paper until the librarian told them to hush up or go outside.

Mr. Paul, Mom's hairdresser, asked if he could have an autographed picture of me to hang in the window of his shop, and the man who owns the little place we always go for pizza asked if he could have one to hang near the pizza oven. People I didn't know waved or smiled at me in town. We got a letter from a local clothing store asking if I'd like to model in a summer fashion show, as well as a long-distance call from a neighbor who had moved away a year and a half ago asking if that girl with the braid could possibly be little Sunday, who used to have braces on her teeth and band-aids all over her knees and elbows. A lady Mom met at a party around Christmas called to ask if she thought her son could model, too, and did we have connections, and I got a phone call from a mystery man who said he wanted to meet me and take me out for a night I'd never forget. Mom turned white when I told her and said we were going to have to get an unlisted number.

Then a straw-paper came sailing at me in the cafeteria one day, followed by Stewart, who ambled over, tossed my almost-empty milk carton into the dead-center of the garbage pail, and pulled up a chair. Right out of—yes!— left field, he asked, "Are you going on the moonlight sail with anyone in particular?"

I felt as if he'd hurled *me* through the air. I felt as if

I were sailing off the ground at a hundred miles an hour. "No, nobody in particular."

The truth was, Karen had alerted me that Bim was going to ask me and so were about half the boys in the eighth grade. The problem was, no one had been able to get up the nerve. I was the hot celebrity of Stanhope Junior High and the guys were suddenly too nervous to approach me. Karen said I'd become an "awesome luminary."

"In that case, *I'll* take you," Stewart said, and he tipped back his chair so far I thought he was going to slam backward onto the vinyl tile.

"Fine," I said, hoping I didn't sound as if a hand grenade were exploding in my stomach, which is how I felt.

"Okay, we're on then," Stewart said, and he tipped his chair into normal position, got up, and loped off.

I danced home. I heard music in my head that was coming from nowhere. Stewart and me, me and Stewart. Under the stars. Over the water. If this is what it meant to be a celebrity, okay, I'd take it!

When I got home, Mom and Edward were weeding together. Edward was sneezing. I said nothing. I just stared at the new grass and the old grass and the weeds and the bushes and the fence that needs two new slats, and I thought I'd never seen anything as beautiful as our front yard. "God bless you! Gesundheit!" I said to Edward. I danced inside and drank some fruit juice, and when the glass left a wet ring on the kitchen table, I made a little heart out of the ring. Wait until I told Karen. Wait until I told the world!

While I dialed Karen's busy number, I took a ballpoint and wrote "Stewart and Sunday" on the inside of my notebook—twice with my right hand, once with my left hand, once upside down, and once in mirror writing, which didn't turn out well. Karen seemed to have taken the phone off the hook or was playing her favorite record albums to someone on the other end. I would try again after dinner.

Dinner was delicious. Dessert was delicious. Edward had stopped eating desserts, just like that—after his fish died. Now he really was trim. I thought he looked like a very handsome little boy. Funny I hadn't noticed how good-looking he was before this. "You look better than a real king," I said.

"You look better than a real Jack," he answered.

"Don't fight, kids," Mom said.

Fight? I wanted to sing! I went into my room and closed the door and put The Heartfelt Four on the stereo and Essence de Mer behind my ears and started dialing Karen's number again.

At last!

"Karen, you know how long I've been trying to get you? Did you take the phone off the hook?"

"No, I've been talking to Erin, and she's in a bad way. I mean, really *down*. I was trying to cheer her up."

Something in me lurched. "Really? What's wrong?"

"It's Stewart. Maybe I shouldn't say this to you, but he's a real *loser*. You know what he did?"

I caught my breath. I wanted to hear it, I didn't want to hear it. "What did he do?"

"You won't believe this, Sun! He made a date with her for the moonlight sail and then, without any good reason, he canceled out. He said he'd changed his mind. Like that —pffft."

"You're kidding."

"No! Poor Erin! He really bent her out of shape!"

"Karen, he asked *me* to go with him."

"*When?*"

"Today!"

"The rat!"

"Why would he do that, Karen? Ask Erin first and then, just like that, change his mind?"

"He asked her way back at the snow-shoveling party, but then, when you became a famous person overnight, I guess he thought going with you would make him look pretty big with the guys on the team. You are *the* status symbol now. After all, you're the star of the school, Sunday!"

The star of the school hung up and walked downstairs. The music in my head was off. Mom was in front of the television with the newspaper in her lap, and she patted a place on the couch next to her for me to sit down. "I'll bet you'll be coming up on this channel at the station break.

I have a hunch that right after this game show, you'll be on. Mmm, you smell nice."

"What happened to Arizona?" I asked. My collarbone was starting to throb; rain tomorrow. Maybe rain forever. "Are we moving or not?"

"Dad says he's willing to put it off until September. We'll make a decision then. He's not a selfish man, Sunday, and I think he realizes it would be *crazy* to interrupt your career." Mom had put on her glasses to read the paper, so I couldn't really see her eyes. She was sort of trying to look over them at me. "And this summer, who knows, I might take Edward down to the city and have some professional photographs made of *him*."

"Edward! Not Edward!"

"He's lost so much weight, dear. Haven't you noticed how *adorable* he's become?"

From Edward's room, which faces the front of the house, I could see right out to the front lawn. It was still light, and I could see it very clearly—the shrubs, the grass, even the weeds.

It looked very scruffy, especially where the fence was missing two slats, and what had been so green three hours ago now looked all faded and seedy. "Hey, Edward, may I borrow your new scissors?" I asked.

He wasn't using them and never had, except to cut out the picture of me from the paper and paste it in his scrapbook. Now he was lying on his stomach on his bed, reading a comic book.

"You're gonna forget to bring 'em back."

"I won't."

"You will."

"I won't."

"Okay, but you better not. They're good scissors. And you never know. You may get in the paper again."

I took them to my room and closed the door. My hand was really shaking, which surprised me. Stop shaking, chicken, I said to myself, and I lifted my hand with the scissors in them and it was absolutely a miracle—my hand turned perfectly steady and firm, as if I'd slipped a cast over it.

I never hesitated, but it wasn't easy, and I don't think I did the best job.

Mr. Paul would definitely have done it differently. I just held my braid straight up in the air and scissored it off. Then I took the cut-off piece, and after looking at it for a minute, staring at the length of it, I tossed it across the room into the wastebasket near my dresser. It missed. No perfect shot.

I ran my fingers through my leftover hair and checked myself out in the mirror. I sort of liked my choppy, un-even, crazy haircut. I was a different/strange/short-haired person, a new, less adorable but perfectly decent me.

"Welcome back, ordinary Sunday," I said to my face in the mirror.

To Edward, I said, "I'm returning your scissors," as I stopped in his room on my way to the hall telephone, and he didn't even look up. He didn't know that I might be saving him from having to be a dynamite kid. He was too sensitive for the Gray Beards of this world. He deserved to be allowed to stay the ordinary little pest he was. "I love you, my poor fishless brother," I added, but I don't think he heard me.

I didn't have to look up Stewart's number. I had it memorized from having looked at it about twenty times in the telephone book, just in case I ever needed to call it—like now.

Not necessary to tell my hand to stop shaking when I lifted the receiver this time. I was a rock. Stewart was somewhere in the basement, his mother said, so I had to wait for what seemed like two years before he picked up the telephone.

"Stewart?"

"How ya doin'?"

"It's Sunday." I thought about all those Stewart and Sunday's I'd written all over my notebook not two hours ago and wished they'd all fade out fast, like the front lawn.

"What's up?"

"I'm afraid I won't be able to go on the moonlight sail with you." Considering it was still a month away, I actually could have waited until tomorrow to tell him, couldn't I? No. I had to do it now, this minute.

"Yeah? How come?"

"I changed my mind," I said, hoping he'd get the point, and ice practically covered the receiver.

"Well, no prob," he said, "It's okay." His voice sounded exactly the way it always did. The force of my storm obviously did not blow him away or bury him in an avalanche; it didn't even seem to give him a chill. But when we hung up, I felt better than better. I felt really good.

I squared my shoulders and walked downstairs, pretty slowly, getting my courage together. Mom was just where I'd left her, in the den, in front of the television set. When I walked in, she squinted, then tore off her glasses.

"Good lord, Sunday! Oh, no! Honey, your hair! What have you *done*?" she cried.

When I saw the look on her face, I thought I might panic, but I didn't. I said, "Mom, don't worry. It'll all grow back someday."

"It'll all grow back someday—?" It was as if she'd recorded the words in her head as I said them but was just slowly getting the meaning now.

"I'm sorry. I just *had* to, Mom."

"Your braid, gone!"

"Yeah."

"Your career—"

"I guess it's over."

Mom's silences hang in the air like big mushroom clouds. This one seemed to take up all the space and make it hard to breathe. Until she got up suddenly and touched my hair as if she had to convince herself half of it was really gone. She stood there a minute looking as if she were going to spin off the floor, scream, or throw an ashtray through the window. Instead, she just shook her head.

"It's over," I repeated, and she blinked.

Then she seemed to recover a little, as if someone had put something under her nose to sniff, and the mushroom cloud was gone.

"It's what you really wanted, dear?"

I nodded.

"I'll get used to it. Don't worry, Sunday. I know I will," she said, but she kept shaking her head back and forth as if it might take ten or twenty years.

I remembered again that advice the lady in the banana shirt gave me at the peanut butter commercial last fall: Smile if it *kills* you.

It wasn't easy this time, but I did.

About the Author

Marlene Fanta Shyer's previously published
books for young readers include *Tino, Blood in
the Snow, My Brother, the Thief,* and *Welcome
Home, Jellybean* (also available from
Scholastic). She has contributed fiction to
*Good Housekeeping, McCall's, Ladies' Home
Journal,* and other magazines, and is the
author of two novels for adults, *Local Talent*
and *Never Trust a Handsome Man.* Ms. Shyer
lives in Larchmont, New York, with her
family.